Book Town: A Novel

Paul Combs

The Stratford Press
USA

ALSO BY PAUL COMBS

The Last Word

Writer in Residence

Book Town: A Novel

Copyright © 2018 by Paul Combs. All rights reserved.

Printed in the United States of America

ISBN-13: 978-0692142998
ISBN-10: 0692142991

Published by The Stratford Press

10 9 8 7 6 5 4 3 2 1

First Edition

For my girls, and for Indi. No retreat, no surrender.

"Every book has a soul, the soul of the person who wrote it and the soul of those who read it and dream about it." – Carlos Ruiz Zafon, *The Shadow of the Wind*

1

"Therapy"

"I think I'm starting to miss killing people."

Silence. She taps on her coffee mug with the end of her pen, which Jake Donovan has often seen her do when she's searching for something profound to say. It isn't a new subject; in the past he's brought it up as a way to avoid talking about other things.

At previous meetings Dr. Jenret had suggested that he had never really enjoyed killing people, which was probably true, but rather that the military had given him a sense of belonging to something and that was what he missed. He expects a similar response this time, but doesn't really care either way. He's here as much out of habit as anything else.

While she mulls over a response, he smooths his collar and glances around the office. She has transitioned from a Far Eastern theme to an African one. Tribal drums have replaced statues of the Buddha, and prints of elephants and water buffalo hang where Japanese silk screens previously adorned the walls. Only the incense burners remain, on the small bookcase. It's still more calming than the Aztec/Maya/Inca décor that dominated the room on his first visit. Prints of pyramids are fine, but the ceremonial stone knife on a miniature Aztec sacrificial altar was a bit much.

"I think you have anger management issues," she says. Now that's a new direction, one he didn't see coming.

"I think I should backhand you for that," he says.

She laughs. Her pale blue eyes sparkle, and it makes her even more attractive than usual. She's wearing a skirt that displays her shapely, tanned legs, and he briefly considers suggesting again that having sex with her will stimulate his "progress." This approach has failed several times over the past year, as he expected it would, but Jake doesn't discourage easily.

"You won't hit me, if for no other reason than the fact that I'm the only therapist in this town who will have anything to do with you."

She has him there. You dangle one egghead with a Lenin beard over a third-floor balcony railing and word gets out to the psychiatric community pretty quickly. Plus, he has never struck a woman. Shot a few, but never struck one.

"Maybe I'm just depressed. I heard somewhere that anger is often depression turned outward." See what her massive psychiatric ego does with that one.

"Perhaps," she replies. "But you have no symptoms of depression. In your case, I think it's more likely frustration turned outward."

Frustration? he thinks. *Frustration is trying to casually stand with an erection.*

"An interesting thought," he replies, rising slowly from the chair. "And one I would love to explore more deeply, but I have to preach in forty-five minutes."

Jake always gets nervous before he preaches. We're not talking about your fifth-grade violin recital nervous or asking a girl to prom nervous. No, this is a combination of fear and dread that cannot be adequately explained to someone who has never stood before a large group of people, many of whom heard their first sermon decades before he was born, and presume to speak on behalf of the Creator of the Universe. Pitching the seventh game of the World Series naked and blindfolded seems an easier task, at least to him.

It may also come as a surprise that the size of the audience doesn't play much part in the level of terror he feels. In fact, he is usually calmer, and preaches better in front of a very large congregation. Maybe there is more anonymity in a large crowd, even if you are standing alone before it. Go figure.

The congregation this late Saturday afternoon is, by Baptist standards, huge. The average size of a Southern Baptist church in the United States is 50 members, and a church is considered large if it has 1000 members. Briarwood Baptist has 35,000 members, and therefore has attained the pinnacle every pastor hopes to reach: the megachurch. Not that there are 35,000 in the building at the moment; the sanctuary only holds 10,000, which is why they run four services each weekend. The Saturday afternoon service is popular with the younger members, as it doesn't interfere with their evening plans and leaves plenty of time for on Sunday morning for sleeping in before the tailgating starts prior to kickoff.

Jake is not the pastor of Briarwood; he is the Minister of Outreach and Staff Evangelist, which means he leads mission trips and holds revivals and any number of things the senior pastor has neither the time nor the people skills to handle. This afternoon he is the guest speaker, and as his nerves threaten to drive him back to the comfort of his truck, or even the couch in Dr. Jenret's office, the sanctuary is overflowing, and even more are watching a live video feed in the gym. It's still not the largest crowd he has spoken to. That honor goes to a Sunday night service in Caracas, Venezuela a year or so ago. That night over 95,000 people packed a soccer stadium to listen to him preach, the vast majority not understanding a single word. He had to trust that his translator was accurately conveying his words to them and not simply reciting the recap of Venezuela's win over Paraguay in World Cup qualifying earlier that week. It sounds crazy, but translators had done weirder things when he preached overseas.

It was that triumph in Caracas that ultimately led him to Briarwood, one of the crown jewels of the Baptist world and the largest church in the state of Texas. Until then he had led small trips overseas and held revivals in churches with far fewer than the average size of 50 members. He had his retirement pay from the Army to supplement his meager income, but his new rock star status and relative youth enticed the Briarwood's Senior Pastor, Stephen Campbell, to bring him on staff full-time.

The praise band plays the final notes of whatever song they have been playing (he never notices the last song before stepping up to the pulpit) and the choir files off the platform. Jake rises and steps to the podium, not even bothering to open his Bible. One advantage of being an evangelist is that you basically give the same sermon over and over; just ask Billy Graham. At that moment, he would have much rather been in a bookstore.

At roughly the same moment, Sal Terranova would rather have been anywhere *but* at The Last Word, the bookstore he owns with his cousin, Camden Templeton. And while Jake is dealing with jitters in front of a huge crowd, Sal is battling an army of two: Camden and Julia Hall, who happens to be both his best employee and his girlfriend.

"You have to admit that you've been slacking off lately," Camden says in her normal I-know-better-than-you-about-everything voice. Not surprisingly, Julia takes a more tactful approach.

"I know you enjoyed having Max around," she says, referring to an author who had taken up residence with them for a brief time but had since moved into his own apartment, "and I know better than both of you that bookselling has its less than exciting moments. But we need you around here, Sal."

"There is nothing here you need me for that Ben or Heather or one of the Sirens can't handle," he says defiantly. "I've become a glorified clerk."

"And what exactly does that make me?" Julia snaps, all attempt at tact vanished in an instant. "I do the same job as you, but whereas you're an owner, I'm just an employee." She doesn't wait for answer; after throwing him a withering look she storms off to the back of the store.

Sal turns to Camden, expecting more abuse, but she has apparently decided that nothing needs to be added. She shrugs, and then walks to the back herself.

"You're an idiot," says a voice behind Sal. He turns to see Jacob Weinberg, the store's septuagenarian Rare Books expert.

"Don't you start too, Jacob" Sal says, his shoulders slumping. "I'm not really in the mood to hear about what a noble profession we're in and all that rah-rah crap."

"It is a noble profession," Jacob says, "a lot more noble than what you were doing before. But that's not why you're an idiot."

"Oh? Then why am I an idiot?"

"If you don't know, me telling you won't help. Just don't forget Julia was out of your league from the start."

Sal considers this for a moment, then nods. There is no way to argue that he would regret losing Julia, though he seems to be doing everything in his power to ensure exactly that outcome. He walks past Jacob and out the front door without another word.

"I rarely find myself defending my idiot cousin," Camden tells Julia, who is absentmindedly rearranging sugar packets on the counter of the break room, "but maybe you should give him a pass for that stupid comment."

"Which one?" Julia asks bitterly. "He makes so many in the course of a day."

"Point taken. But as you said yourself, he misses Max, and there's more than that. First Max leaves, then the city denies his permit for a literary festival downtown."

"Because of the Hemingway fiasco," Julia interrupts, stifling a smile at the memory.

"Yes," Camden says. "Twenty-three drunk Hemingway lookalikes and Sal roaming the streets pretending oncoming cars were bulls to be fought is something the mayor is unlikely to forget for some time."

"If ever."

"And finally there was poor Mr. Moriarty's heart attack. I don't believe his story about a lost manuscript written by Dickens and Dumas hidden somewhere out in the world just waiting to be found, but Sal lives for that kind of quest, and for him to have a heart attack right after leaving our store, and before he could give Sal any details, was a huge disappointment for Sal."

"But Jacob says Mr. Moriarty is doing much better," Julia protests. "Sal will be able to get the whole story at some point, and then he'll probably take off without so much as a goodbye."

"Not the point," Camden says. "The point is that Sal needs big projects. He has the attention span of cocker spaniel except when he has some grand scheme cooking; you know that better than most. And right now he has no schemes."

"Then we have to find him one fast," Julia says. "I don't know how much longer I can put up with surly, sulking Sal."

Outside the store, Sal lights a cigarette in the fading sunlight and looks across the street at the bench where he first asked Julia out more than a year ago. There is an older man sitting there now, and Sal nods at him when they make eye contact. To his surprise, the man motions for Sal to join him.

As he crosses the street, Sal looks more closely at the man. He's short and stocky, maybe in his mid-60s, with an impressive white beard and bald head. He's wearing blue jeans, work boots, and a flannel shirt, which makes him look like a lumberjack. This immediately makes Sal think of Monty Python's "Lumberjack Song," and he is laughing by the time he takes a seat beside the old guy.

"What's so funny, young man?" the guy asks him.

"Sorry," Sal replies. "I was thinking about a Monty Python song."

"Who?"

"Monty Python," he repeats. "You know, the English comedy guys? *Holy Grail, Life of Brian?*" The man stares at him as if he's speaking a foreign language. "It's not important. Why did you call me over here?"

"I just arrived here after a long journey," the man says, "and I'm looking for Irma's Café."

"That's not far," Sal tells him. "You go a few blocks past the courthouse on Main and it's on the left. But they're closed now; they open for breakfast and lunch, but not dinner."

"Ah," the man replies, stroking his beard. "I arrived too early."

"Yeah," Sal says. "About 12 hours too early."

"I will need to return later then," he answers after a lengthy pause. But I do have two words for you."

"Yeah?" Sal asks as he bends over to stub out his cigarette on the pavement, thinking immediately of the two words he has most often heard and doubting the old man means those. "What two words?"

"Book Town, Salvatore Terranova," he says. "Book Town."

As he straightens up, Sal realizes he never told the old man his name. He can't ask him about it however: the old man is gone.

2

"Sal's Really Bad Day"

When you do business in an urban area, you never know what you'll find with each day's dawning. Most days, Sal finds nothing but order and cleanliness on the sidewalk and street in front of the bookshop, and much the same in the alley in back, because Camden or Julia or Ramon have dealt with the night's leavings long before he has rolled out of bed. Today, however, they are all otherwise engaged, so it falls to Sal to ensure the outside of The Last Word is as attractive as the books inside.

Rising at an hour he sees more as the end of the night than the start of the day is enough to foul his mood. What he finds on this fine, clear morning nearly drives him to violence. Starting at the front of the building (in case he loses interest and decides to stop midway through) he encounters the following items strewn the length of the storefront and beyond: five empty Corona bottles and one half-empty Bud Light can (an odd six-pack), a box of Church's Chicken with four drumsticks (each with one bite taken out), the front section of *The Dallas Free Press* from eight days ago, one pink Cowboy boot (size 12), and a purple bra (size DD). Arranged around the bra in a symmetrical pattern are four corn cobs, presumably also from Church's Chicken, none with so much as a stray kernel remaining. *Reminds me of a Saturday night in high school,* he thinks as he sweeps the last cob into a large dustpan and drops it into a bin on wheels. He had laughed when Julia bought the rolling bin; he's not laughing now.

There are fewer items as he moves down the south side of the building along Goliad Avenue, but they are no less diverse. Into the rolling bin go a blue pacifier, a Joni Mitchell cassette tape, a Chinese takeout box (red, with a few grains of fried rice stuck to the bottom), and a small pile of cigarette butts. In all fairness, these could easily be his, as Camden has finally badgered him into not smoking in front of the store. He normally smokes on the bench across the street, but at times the shade here is better.

It's not until he turns into the alley, however, that his irritation morphs into full-blown rage. Just past loose, wind-blown papers and plastic Coke bottles, not far from the back door of the shop and the stairs that lead to the apartment above it, he encounters a man stretched out on the small strip of grass that borders the alley's pavement. Whether he is dead or unconscious or simply asleep Sal cannot tell from this distance. All three are distinct possibilities, as the prone form is surrounded by no fewer than ten Coors Tall-Boys and a disgusting trail of what can only be vomit. Sal thinks he can even see a kernel or two of corn in the festering mess.

Sal's reaction to this tableau might seem completely out of proportion to most people, but most people don't know how often he encountered this scene as a child in Trenton. And though sociologists and various crusaders would drone on and on about the lack of mental healthcare, unfair economic conditions, and unfortunate drug addiction that left many on the streets, for a ten-year-old kid (even one as tough as he already was) these street denizens were terrifying, causes be damned.

Sal is instantly transported back to the old neighborhood, where Crazy Edgar walked an eight-block circuit all day, every day, muttering to himself about IBM and the devolution of the human soul, and Annie the Cart Lady collected only bottles that were green, and Little Guido (to differentiate him from the non-homeless Big Guido) constantly asked for a quarter and cursed you if you gave him a dollar instead. But it was Syracuse Sally who had forever changed his outlook on street people, in part because they shared the same name and young Sal feared such a fate, but mostly because of one incident that he could never forget.

Sal was walking home with his new skateboard one summer night when Syracuse stepped from behind a dumpster, smacked him in the side of the head with a plank from an old pallet, and made off with the skateboard. Sal had not lost consciousness, but it had hurt like hell and drawn a little blood. His tears were as much over the loss of his prized possession as from pain.

He got the board back, of course. Before Syracuse Sally had even tried to pawn it for enough cash for a bottle of Strawberry Hill, Sal had told his father. It was perhaps a sign of the level of Syracuse's mental illness that even knowing who Mr. Terranova was and Who He Was With, he had still attacked his only son. Less than an hour later Sal had his skateboard back and Syracuse Sally was never seen again. Young Sal had never asked his father what happened; even at that age he knew not to ask. He did know that the punishment far exceeded the crime; he knew it then and he knew it now. But some scars never completely heal, and some change you.

All this flashes through his mind in a split-second as he stands over the inert form in the alleyway. Without even realizing it, during this brief reminiscence he has drawn the Glock from the small of his back and is aiming it directly at the man's head. He notices the gun and ponders his options. He can easily claim self-defense, even with his less-than-spotless record. Better still, he can simply finish the man and call Ortiz, who will spirit the body and all evidence to parts unknown; he certainly would not be missed.

Sal cocks the hammer, and as the sharp metallic click echoes loudly in the silent alleyway, he hears a very unexpected voice in his head:

"Murdering sleeping men behind the bookstore," Julia's voice whispers, "is bad for business. And I would be disappointed in you."

Sal blinks rapidly a few times, looks over his shoulder, then carefully lowers the hammer. He sticks the pistol back in his waistband, pulls out his cell phone, dials 311, and tells the dispatcher that there is a homeless man passed out behind The Last Word Bookstore. After sweeping up the beer cans he heads back to the front of the shop. He leaves the vomit trail as a present for the cops.

Two cups of coffee and a stack of pancakes should have been enough to wash away the unfortunate start to Sal's day. They don't even come close. Four hours after the shop opens he is staring at exactly $8.66 in sales – for a used copy of *Gravity's Rainbow* – when the lone customer in the shop, a well-dressed woman in her sixties, decides to share her opinion of a book they have on display.

"I thought this one was just terrible," she says, pointing at a copy of Somerset Maugham's *The Razor's Edge*. She grins broadly as she says it, as if she knows this is one of his favorite books. Before he can respond, she continues. "But at least it's not as bad as that other one, the one with all the drinking and parties and such." She begins waving her arms around like a giant bird, as if this will help him figure out the title; he already has.

"*The Great Gatsby*?" he asks.

"That's the one!" she exclaims. "So silly, don't you think?"

"I actually think it's one of the greatest novels ever written in the English language," he replies, but she is not listening.

"The absolute worst one," she says, rubbing her chin thoughtfully, "was one they made me read in high school. A guy gets up in the morning and pees off the side of a dock. And they called that literature."

"You can't mean *The Old Man and the Sea*," he says, realizing too late that Heather has overheard the conversation. She flies at the unsuspecting woman's blind side like a linebacker out of a blitz package, but just before impact Julia throws a perfect side body block, knocking Heather halfway across the fiction section.

The woman, who has no clue any of this has happened, walks to the counter, puts several books in front of Sal, pays, and leaves. Once she is gone, Julia and Heather join him, Heather muttering threats and Julia smiling sweetly. Sal looks at the register tape.

"I knew that my dignity and self-respect had a price," he says. "I just figured it was more than $53.99."

"It's worth more than that," Julia says, "once you add sales tax."

3

"An Unexpected Encounter"

Monday is usually a day off for Jake, which is only right since he works Saturday evenings and Sunday mornings. There are times when a day off is impossible: people get sick and hospital visits must be made, a mother urgently needs to speak to him about her 18-year-old daughter who has run off with the drummer of a pop-punk band, a deacon's son decides he's a Buddhist. A minister, even if he's mainly an evangelist, is on call 24 hours a day.

Happily, on this fine Monday there are no pressing demands, so he is free to go wherever the spirit leads him, as the saying goes. This morning the spirit leads him to Irma's Café for a breakfast of bacon, eggs, hash browns, and biscuits and gravy. You can't appreciate the joy of being alone unless you almost never are.

Irma's had survived every change the city went through from 1943 to the present day, and would surely outlive him. He slides into his usual booth, orders, and doesn't bother trying to read the paper until after he has finished breakfast and started on his third cup of coffee. Prior to that it would have been a futile effort, as everyone in the café feels compelled to stop by his table to say good morning, compliment him on Saturday's sermon, or ask how he thought the Cowboys would do this year. This last thing has always amazed Jake, but he supposed that since they were God's Team, people assumed he would have inside information.

He is deep into a story about the reemergence of Russia as a world power, wondering why the writer seems so shocked by this development, when a man stops beside his booth. Jake doesn't look up at first, frankly hoping the man will just move on when he sees that he is reading. The man doesn't move on, however, and does not speak. Jake finally looks up from the paper and is taken aback, for though he has never seen this man before, there is an overwhelming feeling of familiarity about him.

He is a small man, perhaps 65 years old, barely five-foot-six, bald, and sturdily built, as if he has spent his life doing manual labor; his lined, weathered face confirms that he has spent a great deal of time outdoors. He is quite bow-legged, with a long nose, white beard, and eyebrows that nearly meet. Had he not been wearing blue jeans, a flannel shirt, and work boots Jake would swear he was a character from a Renaissance painting, one of those with a Biblical theme.

The stranger still does not speak, just stares at Jake intently for longer than is comfortable. It is Jake who breaks the silence.

"Can I help you, sir?" he asks, reluctantly setting the paper aside.

"Actually, John Kennedy Donovan," he replies a rich baritone, "it is I who am here to help you."

"Help me?" he asks. He isn't surprised that a stranger would know his name. When you serve on the staff of a huge church and have a weekly radio show, a lot of people know who you are.

"Yes, help you," the old man repeats. "Are you going to ask me to sit down, or is hospitality as dead in your time as I have heard?"

With a statement like that Jake is tempted to send him on his way and go back to reading the paper, but now he is also intrigued. He gestures to the seat opposite him and the stranger slides into the booth. The way he eyes the remnants of Jake's breakfast makes him think this whole thing is nothing more than a ploy to grab a free meal, and Jake is accustomed to this as well. From gasoline to get to Midland, to diapers, to a bottle of whiskey, people are constantly asking him for money for one thing or another.

"Have you eaten?" Jake asks him, as pleasantly as he can; the line about hospitality had actually bothered him, having grown up with that old "entertaining angels in disguise" line drilled into him.

"Not in a very long time," he replies with a sly smile. He doesn't look malnourished, but it's hard to tell. Jake motions the waitress over and she hands him a menu. He looks up at Jake.

"What do you suggest?" he asks.

"Can't go wrong with bacon and eggs," Jake answers. "The pancakes are good too."

"What animal does bacon come from?"

Now that is an odd question, but maybe he's a turkey bacon kind of guy.

"A pig," the waitress answers, more sweetly than she had spoken to Jake earlier. Being older has its benefits. "We sometimes have deer bacon, but it's not in season."

"No pork of any kind," he says firmly. "I will have eggs and pancakes, please. And some of that black beverage he is drinking."

"Coffee," she says helpfully. She walks back to the counter and returns with the pot and a mug for him. She refills Jake's cup as well, but only after he asks. Maybe he had said something in a sermon that offended her.

"You obviously know my name," Jake says after giving him sugar and cream for his coffee. "What's yours?"

"Saul," he says. "But you can call me Paul if you like. I answer to either." His eyes twinkle at this, most likely in response to the expression on Jake's face.

"Saul," Jake repeats. "Or Paul. Like the apostle?"

"Very much like the apostle," he says with a nod. "In fact, the very same."

Wonderful, Jake thinks. It is just his luck to encounter a lunatic on his day off. God is punishing him for something, like the fact that he still drinks beer or because of the language he too often uses on Dallas freeways.

"I understand your skepticism," the man continues. "It's not every day that an apostle shows up at your breakfast table."

"It doesn't happen *any* day," Jake says. "And after you finish eating you should probably get to a counselor or something. I know a good one who would love to talk to you, though she'll probably just say you have anger management issues." He stands up and places some money on the table. "Enjoy your breakfast." As he turns to walk out the door the man speaks again, in a voice so soft Jake barely hears him.

"If you didn't want me to come," he asks, "then why have you been praying so hard for answers?"

Normally Jake would have just kept walking. Delusional people sometimes say things that are just generic enough to keep your attention. He was a preacher, for crying out loud; of course he prayed for answers. But there is something in the man's tone that makes him stop in spite of himself. He sits back down.

"I know I'll regret asking this, because all it will do is waste more of my day off, but what answers are you talking about?"

"Answers to the Questions, the big ones that have been bothering you so much you aren't sleeping."

"I've had insomnia since I was 14 years old," Jake says. "Pretty good guess, though I'm sure I've mentioned it in sermons before. You'll have to do better than that."

He smiles and takes a sip of his coffee. The plate of eggs and pancakes is empty; apparently it has been a while since he's last eaten.

"You have doubts about being part of such a large church," he says, "and are concerned about the direction it's going. You even question your calling."

"That describes anyone in a leadership position in a large organization," Jake says with a laugh. "You could say the same to a CEO or baseball manager and be correct to some degree."

"True," he agrees with a nod. "But CEOs and baseball managers, whatever those are, don't lie awake at night worrying about what an old Venezuelan priest said to them in Caracas the morning before they preached to a stadium full of people."

They say that a heart attack feels like someone hitting you in the chest with a hammer. If Jake ever has one, at least he'll know what to expect, such is the effect of this statement on him.

"How do you know that?" he demands. He intends it as a shout; it comes out as a whisper. "I never told anyone about that."

"But you did pray about it," the stranger says with an understanding smile. "You've prayed about it for a long time."

"Not to you," Jake says, not even realizing that he is suddenly treating this old, delusional man like he is indeed the second coming of the Apostle Paul. "I only pray to God, not to saints."

He smiles as if this is quite amusing to him.

"Actually, no one 'prays' to the saints," he says, in a voice you might use with a preschooler. "But that's a different conversation. And of course you prayed to God. Who do you think told me?"

Now Jake knows he's a lunatic: he thinks God speaks to him. But how did he know about the priest?

The incident that Jake had been praying about, that this man inexplicably knew about, had indeed happened during that fateful mission trip to Caracas. He was sitting at an outdoor café, going over his sermon for that night, when a priest old enough to have travelled with the real Saint Paul approached his table. In spite of his age he seemed in good health and his eyes had fire in them. He did not introduce himself, or even wait for Jake to speak, before challenging him in good if slightly broken English.

"Why do you come here to convince other Christians that your Christianity is more valid than theirs?" he demanded.

It certainly seemed a fair question. The honest answer would be that most Baptists didn't consider Catholics to be Christians, but that would sound arrogant, so Jake just smiled and handed him a tract on the real way to a

23

relationship with Christ. He doubted that the priest would stay for his sermon.

"Do you even care that the instant relationship with Jesus you offer does nothing to improve the lives of these people?" he asked, tucking the tract into his pocket for later scrutiny. "You preach about salvation in the next life while they starve to death in this one. You should try reading James 2:14-17." He stormed away down the boulevard, not giving me a chance to respond.

Well, the joke was on him, because Jake knew what the passage said. In a nutshell, it said that faith without deeds was dead, and as best he could tell had nothing to do with him. After all, wasn't he putting his faith to work being here, thousands of miles from home, telling people about Jesus?

That should have been the end of it. Lord knows he had dealt with worse abuse than that over the years, and hecklers with more detailed arguments. But the old priest's words had stuck with him. Hardly a week passed that he didn't dream about the encounter. And yes, he had prayed that the dreams and the unease about the whole thing would pass. He never spoke of it to anyone, and yet this old fraudster knew. How?

"How do you know about the priest?" Jake asks again.

"As I said, I was told about it before I was sent here."

"Really? And what else were you told?"

24

"Only what I need to know to get by and fulfill my mission," he says in a matter-of-fact tone. "Not nearly enough, really. I know a little about you, and your dream, and some practical things like how to dress so I don't stand out and that this is a place called America, but nothing about baseball or bacon."

Something suddenly occurs to Jake.

"How is it I can understand you?" he asks. "Shouldn't you be speaking Aramaic or Greek or even Latin?"

"But I am speaking Aramaic. God must have given you the ability to speak and understand it. It's a miracle!"

"Seriously?"

"No," he says with a mischievous laugh. "I'm just messing with you. Apparently, he gave me the ability to speak English. Sorry."

This is going nowhere, and Jake is about to just leave in spite of what the man seems to know about him, when he catches something the man had said.

"You said you know about my dream," Jake says. "What dream are you talking about?"

"The one about the priest in Venezuela, of course. Haven't you been listening?"

"No, you first said you knew I had prayed about it, not dreamed about it."

"And part of the reason you're praying is you can't get the dream to stop," he says. His eyes are intent upon Jake.

"Every week, the same café, the same priest, the same conversation. And when you wake, the same doubt. It would bother me too."

Jake sits speechless. Maybe the stranger isn't insane; maybe he is. Maybe he has simply cracked and the guy isn't here at all. Because if he is, Jake has to now consider the possibility, however remote, that he is sitting in a booth having coffee with the Apostle Paul.

"I am not a lunatic," he says as if reading Jake's mind, "and you're not going crazy. I have a few more things I'm allowed to do to prove who I am, but I don't want to use them unless I have to. For now, how about you and I go see something I've heard about."

"What's that?" Jake asks.

"A bookstore."

"A bookstore?" Jake repeats, not sure he has heard correctly.

"Yes," he says. "A bookstore."

4

"God's Marketplace"

It's just a short drive north from Irma's Café to The Last Word, which is the first bookstore Jake thinks of. It's also a good place to go since he knows people there; maybe they can help him figure out what to do with this poor old man. He had no worries about letting the stranger into his truck, since he was confident he could subdue him if necessary. After all, he is twenty years younger, at least six inches taller, and fifty pounds heavier. Furthermore, like any good Texan preacher, he's armed.

The store is just opening when they arrive, and Camden, Sal, and Heather are the only ones there. Since he is not comfortable announcing to them that he is driving the Apostle Paul around Fort Worth this morning, Jake introduces him as his uncle from Palestine. They naturally assume he means the little town in East Texas, and not the Holy Land. He has barely finished the introductions before the old man rushes over to a section marked "Religion." Heather and Jake follow him.

"Can I help you find something specific?" Heather asks politely.

"I am not sure, young lady," he says. "I have heard stories of stores filled with Bibles and religious books, but this doesn't seem like very many."

"Because of limited shelf space we only carry a small selection of Bibles," she explains. "We also have the Upanishads, the Vedas, and the Tibetan Book of the Dead, but religious books don't sell that well here."

"Why is that?" Jake asks.

"Most people like to buy their Bibles at a Christian bookstore," she says.

Jake feels like an idiot. Of course that's what most people do; it's what he does. Even the small bookstore at Briarwood has ten times the number of Bibles they have at The Last Word.

"Right," he says. "If I had known my...um, uncle, was looking for Bibles I would have gone there."

"Let's go now," Paul says. He is very insistent for a supposed saint.

"Okay," Jake says. Clearly he is not getting rid of the guy yet. "Anyone else want to come along? Seems pretty dead in here right now."

"Mondays start slow," Camden tells him. "It will pick up."

"I'll go with you," Heather says. Camden raises an eyebrow and Sal stifles a laugh.

"Sure," Sal says, "just be back before the lunch rush." He turns to Jake. "You'll be safe enough. They don't carry Hemingway at the Christian stores. And by the way, I actually met your uncle the other night. He moves quick for an old man."

Jake has no idea what he is talking about, on either point, but is glad Heather is going with them. They recently started dating, after some match-making by Julia, but their schedules conflict a lot more than he would like. She would probably not be at all shocked if Saul told her who he is.

The closest Christian bookstore is west of downtown off Hulen Street, and it advertises itself as the largest Christian store in the world. Jake figures this will impress his guest more than the few shelves he saw at The Last Word. Heather is in the passenger seat, Saul in the back.

As they drive west on I-30, Saul (he seems to prefer that to Paul for some reason) marvels at the cars, the overpasses, the buildings, pretty much everything he sees. This surprises Heather, though Jake says nothing.

"Not like Palestine, huh?" Heather asks at one point.

"Rome was incredible to behold," he says. "But even at the height of the Empire it was nothing like this. There were many wonderful buildings of stone and marble, to be sure, but most of the city was made up of narrow streets and cramped wooden row houses stacked on top of each other. It wasn't until after the fire that it truly became grand, and as you know, I didn't live long after the fire."

Heather stares at back at him, then looks over at Jake. He shrugs as if to say *my uncle's a little eccentric*, but he also feels a little bad for the guy. Even if he was simply schizophrenic, it was rude to remind someone of their own death, imagined or otherwise.

They exit at Hulen Street, go left across the overpass, and then turn immediately right into a large shopping center. To their left is a Whole Foods Market, to the right a strip of boutiques and restaurants. Directly in front of them is the store they are looking for, taking up who knew how many thousand square feet of prime retail space, all in the service of the Lord.

Jake parks the truck and they are almost inside when Saul stops suddenly, gazing up at the huge neon letters forming the name of the store. Jake thinks he is once again marveling at modern architecture; he is mistaken.

"You have got to be kidding!" he exclaims. For someone supposedly new to the 21st century, he has some of the lingo down pretty well. He smacks his forehead with his open palm, and rocks back and forth a little. Heather looks at Jake, alarmed.

"What?" Jake asks, having no idea what set him off.

"The name," he shouts, pointing up at the sign. People are beginning to stare.

Jake looks up at the name of the store, even though he knows it very well already. He has been coming here for years and it has never had such an effect on him. How could a simple name matter? Then he sees it from Saul's perspective.

DAMASCUS ROAD CHRISTIAN SUPERSTORE

"Oh," is all Jake can manage to say, and he ushers Saul inside before he can start yelling.

If the sign had outraged Saul, the inside stuns him. He stands just inside the entrance, staring wide-eyed and open-mouthed at the sheer volume of goods laid out in neat, orderly aisles before him. Jake wouldn't have thought someone who had supposedly walked the markets and bazaars of ancient Corinth, Ephesus, Jerusalem, and Rome would be so overwhelmed by a display of commercial wares. Then again, this much stuff under one roof, all nominally devoted to the spread of the Gospel, actually is a lot to take in.

"I want to go look at the jewelry," Heather says, pointing at several cases of crosses hanging from chains, earrings, and the like.

"Didn't you tell a nun not long ago that that you're a Wiccan?" Jake asks.

"I just did that to see how she would react," she says with a grin. "I'm actually more of an agnostic Methodist.

You two go on, I'll catch up." She bounds away without another word.

Jake decides the best way to handle this little tour is to treat it that way: as a tour. He takes Saul by the arm and steers him to the left, past the checkout counters and toward a wall covered with Bibles. This seems like the best place to begin, for obvious reasons.

"These are the Bibles they have for sale," Jake announces in his best tour-guide voice, and he immediately feels like an idiot. Of course they are Bibles.

"I have never actually seen one of these before," Saul replies, picking up the one closest to him, a fat study Bible in burgundy leather. "I was told this was how the scriptures had been collected, told about books, but in my mind I still saw scrolls."

Jake nods, remembering too late that the book as we know it was centuries from being invented when Saul, the real Saul, was alive.

"But tell me," he says earnestly, "why are there so many?"

"So many?" Jake repeats, not understanding.

"Yes. There would be the Torah and the Prophets and the Writings, and there are the Gospels and the Letters. Surely these do not require so many books to hold them."

"No," Jake says. "Each volume holds the entirety of what you mentioned. But there are different version and editions, depending on what a person prefers."

"I don't understand."

"How much do you know about the history of the Bible, as we have it now I mean?"

"Virtually nothing," he replies. "I was simply made to understand that this is how you read the scriptures today."

"Ok. In a nutshell, here's how it went. Originally, as you know, the Jewish scriptures were in Hebrew, and the Christian scriptures in Greek. Then that all got translated into Latin. After another 1200 years or so it was translated into various languages: German, Spanish, English, etc. As far as the English version, there are now a great many different translations."

"Why would there be different translations for the same language?" he asks. "That hardly makes sense."

"Language changes over the centuries," Jake explains, "so it needed to be updated, for lack of a better word, so people today could understand. The most popular version for centuries, the King James Version, is as foreign to readers today as Shakespeare."

"I like him," Saul says.

"You've read Shakespeare's plays?" Jake asks, surprised.

"The plays are ok," he says. "I meant I like him, as a person. I see him quite often."

"Right." He resists the urge to ask who else he sees quite often, like Elvis or Amelia Earhart. "There is also the issue of translating the original language, Greek or Hebrew, word-for-word or thought-for-thought. Which one you choose alters the way the text reads, if not the actual meaning."

"Sounds very complicated," he says thoughtfully. "Why not just learn Greek and Hebrew, the way Muslims all learn Arabic?"

"Some do," Jake says, wondering how he knew this about Muslims, "but most want to read the Word in their native language."

He nods and picks up a different Bible, this one in a box labeled "The Godly Wife Study Bible." He gives Jake a confused look. Apparently one of the salespeople sees this look and rushes over to assist them.

"Are you looking for a specific Bible?" the young man, whose name tag identifies him as Caleb, asks.

"Until just now I had no idea there was more than one kind," Saul answers with a sardonic smile.

"There are a great many," Caleb says. "Children's Bibles, Student Bibles, Bibles geared toward living a proper Christian life or recovery from addiction, men's study Bibles, apologetics Bibles. The one you are holding, for example, is filled with study notes on how to be the wife God has called you to be."

"I don't think you need that one," Jake says to Saul, taking it and placing it back on the shelf.

"I agree," Caleb says with a short, solicitous laugh. "There are also Bibles for specific careers, like soldiers, firemen, police officers. Pretty much anything you can think of."

"Anything?" Saul asks with a grin. "Do you have one for a two thousand year old apostle?"

Caleb stares at him blankly, and Jake quickly intervenes, giving Saul a sharp look in the process.

"My uncle is a jokester," he says. "And although it might not seem like it, he is quite the scholar. Maybe a good study Bible would be best for him, one with lots of commentary and maybe even some Greek and Hebrew."

Caleb's eyes light up at this, confirming Jake's initial suspicions: he is a seminary student and in his first year of Greek studies.

"I just recently started learning Greek at Seminary," he gushes, "and I have found this Bible to be wonderful."

Jake can hear him capitalize the "S" in seminary. This means he's attending the Southern Baptist Seminary just south of here, the *only* seminary as far as the most Baptists in Texas are concerned. Jake had gone there himself, and certainly wouldn't be on staff at Briarwoood if he hadn't. Jesus probably wouldn't be on staff at Briarwood without attending The Seminary first.

He moves along the wall, stopping midway down to pull down a thick black Bible. Stamped on the front cover in gold letters is "The Interlinear Greek Lexicon Study Bible – King James Version."

"Do you have anything that's not in the King James?" Jake asks. This elicits a skeptical look from Caleb; he is apparently one of those Baptists who believe that since the KJV was good enough for Jesus it should be good enough for us. Jake is just glad the kid hadn't recognized him; thank God for beard stubble and baseball cap.

"You look very familiar, sir," he said as if reading his mind. "Have we met before?"

"I don't think so," Jake says, "but I do come in here a lot."

He nods, looks Jake over one more time, then moves a little farther down the wall, finally pulling down an even bigger black leather Bible. This one is "The Interlinear Greek Lexicon Study Bible – King James Version/New Millennium Readers' Version Parallel Edition." The title barely fits on the cover.

"This Bible has everything the previous one did, as well as the New Millennium Readers' Version alongside the KJV. The NMRV is not meant for serious study, or even for preaching, but it is easier for most people to read for pleasure. I personally haven't used it."

"Thanks," Jake says.

Saul looks at the Bible, weighs its heft in his hands, then turns it over to the back cover. He points at the sticker near the bottom and arches a bushy eyebrow at Jake.

"That's the price," he tells him, looking over at it. "It's $175.00"

"Is that a good price?" he asks.

"This is the Deluxe Leather Edition," Caleb says quickly. "It will last you forever."

Saul nods and looks the Bible over again. Suddenly his eyes flash, as if he has remembered something.

"Caleb, my boy," he says, "do any of these Bible have anything to say about the Apostle Paul's letters?"

Caleb smiles broadly, probably thinking this is another joke. "Of course," he says. "All of them do. But if you really want to delve into Paul's letters you need a standalone commentary. Follow me."

Jake isn't crazy about the idea of Seminary Boy Caleb hijacking his tour, but he follows in silence. If the variety of Bibles had shocked Saul, the Bible Study section might cause him to stroke out, assuming it was physically possible for him to have a stroke, since he'd been dead for two millennia.

The commentaries subsection of the Bible study section of the store takes up three full aisles. Saul gazes up and down the shelves in wonder. There are commentaries on the Old and New Testaments, on the Gospels, on each individual book of the Bible. Caleb leads them to the section containing the commentaries on Paul's letters. Saul bends down to examine some of the volumes, and then looks up quizzically at Jake.

"These all appear to be about the same handful of letters," he says. "What about all the other ones?"

"The letters by the other apostles are a little farther down the shelf," Caleb explains, missing what Jake was pretty sure Saul was asking.

"I think we'll be fine on our own now, Caleb," Jake says politely. "We'll call you if we need anything more. Thanks for your help." He nods and walks away. Jake turns back to Saul. "When you said 'other letters' you didn't mean by other apostles, did you?" he asks.

"Of course not," he says, now down on his knees searching the titles on the lowest shelf. "Where are the rest of *mine?*"

"Were you not filled in on what our Bible contains before you, um, left to come here?" Jake asks. It sounds foolish asking it, since he is still pretty certain this guy is no more the Apostle Paul than he is.

"Of course they did," he replies indignantly. "They said it had four Gospels, Luke's account of our travels —"

"The Acts of the Apostles," Jake says.

"Yes, that. The Revelation of John, which no one seems to understand, some letters by Peter and John and James, and *my* letters."

"The ones you see here are what we have," Jake says.

Saul looks up in astonishment, then back at the shelf, then at Jake again. "But there can't be more than 15 of them if these commentaries include them all," he says, his voice growing louder.

"Calm down," Jake says, glancing around to see if any other customers are nearby and glad to see that Heather is still on the other side of the store. "There are thirteen, actually. Fourteen if you count Hebrews, but there is a good deal of dispute about whether or not you wrote that one."

"Oh please," he says with a derisive snort. "Nicodemus wrote Hebrews. Anyone with half a brain would know that."

"Nicodemus?" Jake asks, shocked. "The member of the Sanhedrin who went to Jesus by night, the one who asked how a man could be born again once he was old? *That* Nicodemus?"

"Yes, that Nicodemus. He knew Jesus, and he was an expert in our Law." He sighs heavily. "Enough about him, where are the rest of my letters?" He almost screams this last sentence. Jake kneels down beside him, placing an arm on his shoulder to try and calm him down.

"How many are missing?" he asks. Saul stares hard at the shelf again.

"Well," he says, thankfully in a much softer voice this time, "I think around seventy or eighty at least."

"Seventy or eighty!" It is an exclamation, not a question, and one customer two aisles away definitely looks over at them. Jake raises his hands in apology. "Are you serious? We're missing more than seventy of your letters?"

"At least," he repeats. "Do you have any of the ones that were sent *to* me?"

"No," Jake answers, "though we do know that the Corinthians sent you at least two, even though we don't have them."

"Two? Try ten. What a pain they were."

This is almost too much for Jake's brain to handle. If true, it means that they had less than 15% of Paul's total correspondence, perhaps much less. What did that mean for how they viewed the early Church? Heck, what did it mean for what they *believe* as the Church?

"What letters of yours are missing?" Jake asks. "Can you tell?"

He thinks about this for a long moment, consulting the names of the letters on the spines of the commentaries. The letters that had been handed down as having been written by Paul were Romans, First and Second Corinthians, Galatians, Ephesians, Philippians, Colossians, First and Second Thessalonians, Philemon, First and Second Timothy, and Titus.

"I assume that when it says 'Romans' it means just one letter, correct?" he asks.

"Yes," Jake says. "When there is more than one, like with Timothy or Corinthians, we numbered them."

"Well then, just off the top of my head I would say you're missing several more to the Romans, about fifteen to Corinth, another three to Ephesus, and some to Timothy and Titus. What is more shocking is that you have none of the ones I wrote to Peter, James and Luke, and the correspondence to Jerusalem, Damascus, Alexandria, Dacia, Gaul, and Spain is all missing."

"Jerusalem?" Jake repeats. "Gaul, Alexandria, and Spain? What was in those letters? Was it different from what we have that remains?"

He stands up and gives Jake a fatherly look, stern yet somehow pleasant.

"How would I know?" he asks. "I don't know exactly which letters you have." He sees Jake's puzzlement and explains. "What I mean is I don't know which of the many letters to Corinth are the two that survived, so I don't know what of importance, if anything, is missing."

"You haven't read them?" Jake asks, incredulous.

"I've been busy," he replies. "You know, being in the presence of the Almighty and all. Get me all of these, and this Bible of course, and I can tell you in a few days."

Jake looks down at the row of commentaries in dismay; it would cost hundreds of dollars for just one set. Fortunately they don't need them. He is a preacher, after all, and every preacher has a reference library.

"I've got plenty back at my place," he assures him. "And more at the church."

"Good. Just the Bible then."

He considers this request. As a staff member of one of the largest congregations in America he is paid well enough that $175 for a Bible will not send him into bankruptcy. But he also has some leeway in ministering to the needs of the community, so he decides to put it on Briarwood's account. They'll even get a discount.

"Done," Jake says, and Saul beams happily at him. Everyone likes getting a new book, especially an expensive one. "Now let me show you the rest of the store." He apparently takes his new job as tour guide quite seriously.

They next move through a small section that sells everything from baptismal robes to communion bread to forms for background checks. In other words, everything a church on the move needs to operate smoothly. Saul seems disinterested in this, other than to ask about the communion bread and the little cups they use for the communion grape juice (500 per box). Jake decides it will be best to explain how the modern version of communion differs from his experience of the Lord's Supper well away from the store; he has already made one scene, and they don't need another.

He walks straight past the section with supplies for parents who homeschool their children, and the area with sheet music also holds no allure for him. When they reach the section with actual CDs, he stops.

"What's this?" he asks, moving his arm in a wide arc around the bins of CDs.

"It's music, all kinds of music, all with a Christian message," Jake answers. "There's Rock, Pop, Country, Rap, basically everything you can get out in the world, but without the bad stuff."

"Bad stuff?"

"Sex and violence and drugs and foul language and Satanism." He clarifies.

"I see. And is the music itself good?"

"Not really. I like a few of the Christian rock bands, though none of them are as good as their secular counterparts." He sighs at the thought. It is true, however; few if any of them could get a record deal with a mainstream record company.

He seems satisfied with this answer and walks over to what was always Jake's favorite area: the children's section. Here there are games and toys and videos and plush stuffed animals, none of which dismembered anything or exploded or glorified demons from the pit. Saul pauses, gets a strange look in his eye, and walks quickly past, stopping at another large section of books.

"Why are there two areas with Bibles?" he asks when Jake catches up to him.

"These aren't Bibles," Jake tells him. "These are regular books, books about how to live a Christian life, biographies, inspirational books, and a lot of Christian fiction."

"Christian fiction? What is fiction?"

"Novels?" Jake offers. Saul stares blankly at him. Jake then remembers that the novel as a form of writing didn't begin for more than a thousand years after his time. "Stories," he says. "Long stories."

"Like the Iliad?" he asks.

43

"Sort of, but not in verse."

"And are these novels as good as their un-Christian counterparts?"

"Non-Christian," Jake corrects, though in truth sometimes his description fits better. "In all honesty, usually not."

Jake had loved books since he was a small child, and he still loved literature. In most cases, Christian fiction was written by people who barely passed Freshman Composition yet found that if they had their one-dimensional character praise Jesus every few pages they could get a book deal with a Christian publishing house.

"Are there not any talented Christian writers?" he asks. It is a valid question.

"There are," Jake answers, "but most of them write books that aren't considered 'Christian' enough for places like this to stock them."

He narrows his eyes.

"What makes them not Christian enough?" he asks. "Bad language, violence, the things you talked about with the music?"

"That's part of it," Jake says. "But it's also the writers themselves who avoid the Christian fiction genre. It has the stigma of not being very good, as far as literary quality or even story quality, so even if they end up being successful within the Christian community, most of the literary world dismisses them."

He ponders this for a while, but says nothing. Jake wonders if he confused him with terms like "literary" and "genre," but doesn't want to embarrass him by asking. He also wonders again why he is even entertaining the possibility that this man is anything other than an escapee from a mental institution.

As they walk over to a large end-cap display, Heather rejoins them. She has picked out several crosses, including a Celtic one.

"I'm going to use this as the model for my next tattoo," she tells Jake. "Want to see where I'm putting it?" This last sentence comes out as a purr. He must have blushed, because she begins laughing and cannot stop for some time.

He quickly turns his attention to the display Saul is examining. It contains all of the latest products related to the new hot thing in the Evangelical world: The Micah 6:8 Prayer. The name, and the prayer, was taken from the Book of Micah in the Old Testament, chapter 6, verse 8 (no one ever said they were creative when it came to naming things). The verse itself said this (from the New Millennium Readers Version):

"The Lord has shown you what is good, as well as what He expects of you. You must always do right to others, be merciful, and walk humbly with your God, obeying Him."

It is a great verse, and had always been a favorite of Jake's. But looking closely at the display, he is suddenly uncomfortable, seeing it the way Saul must. There are paintings of serene landscapes with the words superimposed over them, journals, coffee mugs, key chains, t-shirts, hats, and numerous books, with editions for Bible Study groups, friends, and family. Jake is surprised to see a small Micah 6:8 Study Bible, and how they had chosen a camel and a giraffe as the Micah 6:8 Prayer plush animal mascots is an even greater mystery.

"All this for one passage from Micah?" Saul asks.

"Yeah," Jake answers, a little embarrassed. "We tend to go overboard sometimes."

"Obviously."

"The giraffe is cute, though," Heather says.

They are back at the front of the store now, and there isn't much left to see. They take the Bible to the counter and hand it to the clerk, a young woman of about 20 with a T-Shirt that reads "Damascus Road Christian Superstore: If God Approves of It, We Stock It." She does not seem to disapprove of this version as much as Caleb had. Jake gives her the number of Briarwood's account, and after she applies the discount the total comes to $140.00. There is no tax on Bibles, so today at least they would not be rendering unto Caesar. Jake wondered what Sister Mary Louise would think of that.

"That was an experience," Saul says once they are back in the truck. "To think that in my time we had to hide out in the catacombs, and now you have an entire public market devoted to The Way." He calls Christianity 'The Way,' just like they had back in his time, which Jake thinks is really cool.

"We had better get Heather back to work," Jake says, though in reality he wishes she could stay, and not just so he wouldn't be alone with Saul. He didn't mind really; crazy or not, he is having a good time with the old guy.

When they drop her in front of The Last Word, Heather leans into Jake's window and gives him a long kiss before going back in.

"We need to get together *soon*," she says, then gives Saul a little wave and strolls back into the store. As the truck pulls away, Saul chuckles.

"What's so funny?" he asks.

"You're blushing." Saul answers.

"I don't blush. So where to now?" Jake can see that Saul is thinking hard about this.

"Something bothering you?" he asks.

"I noticed that nowhere in that store did they refer to me as Saint Paul, just Paul or the Apostle Paul," he says. "Why is that? I was led to believe that calling me 'Saint' was common practice."

"For the Saint part we'd need to be in a Catholic bookstore," Jake says with a laugh.

"Oh," he replies with a nod. "Let's go there next then."

"Don't you think you've seen enough of bookstores for one day?"

"Might as well get it all out of the way now."

Jake can't argue with that. There is a Catholic bookstore just east of Downtown, so it is a short drive. But when they get to St. Iraneus Catholic Bookstore it is closed; they are open Tuesday through Saturday. Saul's introduction to the products of the Church of Rome must wait at least one more day.

"So where are you staying?" Jake asks as they cross the bridge heading back downtown.

"No idea," Saul replies. "I just got here, remember?"

Jake thinks this over for several blocks, and then says something that surprises even him.

"Then I guess I have a roommate, at least for tonight."

Saul doesn't say anything, just smiles.

5

"The New Neighbor"

"Looks like we've got some new competition," Ben says as he walks past Sal and Camden at the counter late the next morning. He doesn't elaborate; he simply keeps on walking to a display of Ray Bradbury books that he had set up the night before. He changes the position of several of them. Sal glances at Camden, shrugs, and calls him back over.

"What exactly did that mean?" he asks. He has to keep the conversation focused, because Ben has a habit of running down rabbit trails when he talks, and Camden is virtually unable to form words when Ben is close to her; he looks like a young Adonis. Sadly, for her at least, he is also quite gay.

"What do you think it means?" Ben replies. "A new bookstore; what other kind of competition would we have?"

This is a fair point, but Sal ignores it.

"New bookstore? Where? Why didn't we know about this before now?" As Sal fires off these questions, Camden merely nods, never taking her eyes off Ben.

"You are a very territorial person, Sal," Ben says, "and by that I mean you tend to stick to specific areas almost exclusively. I suppose it's that whole Italian neighborhood back East thing."

"So what?" Sal says, more defensively than he intends.

"So this place is outside your normal, shall we say, comfort zone. It's south of downtown on the edge of the hospital district."

"Ah," Sal says, "where the hipsters live." Sal feels the same way about hipsters that he does about sushi and sweating: avoid whenever possible.

"Yes, Sal," Ben says with an exasperated sigh, "the hipsters are there, along with a lot of young families and a good number of retirees. It is also known by some as the 'gayborhood.'" Sal arches an eyebrow but says nothing. "This guy, though, is not a hipster and so obviously not gay."

"What do you mean 'so obviously not gay?' You can tell who is and who isn't?" Sal asks.

"Not always, no. Just trust me; this guy isn't."

"Where is it exactly?" Camden asks, finally finding her voice and wanting to change the subject. After her experience with her ex-husband, the idea of not being able to tell someone is gay strikes a nerve with her.

"At the corner of Pennsylvania and Jennings. The bookstore takes up one half of the building on the southeast corner; Dino's Subs has the other half."

"I've been down there before," Sal says. "Once, right after I moved here. The subs were ok, not like back home, but ok. The place next door is a nail salon."

"Not anymore," Ben says.

"So did you actually go inside?" Camden asks. "What kind of books does he have?"

"I just stopped in briefly, but his books are, as best I can tell, excellent."

"And ours are crap?" Sal interrupts.

"No, they aren't crap. They are exactly what you expect to find in a good bookstore. His, however, you don't find just anywhere."

"So they're collectible," Camden says. "Like Jacob's books here or the stuff in Randal's store."

"Nope, his books are new, just like ours. But this guy is specializing in literature in translation."

"Foreign language books?" Camden asks, clearly confused now.

"No," Sal says. "Books originally written in a language other than English and translated into English. I know that's a big deal in New York and the West Coast. But I've never heard of anyone doing it down here."

"No one was," Ben says. "Until now."

Ben was right about one thing: Sal is a man who is comfortable in his own neighborhood and at the very least wary anywhere else. Driving south of Interstate 30 on 8th Street, he tenses almost imperceptibly. In his time in Texas he has learned the feel of downtown Fort Worth, its rhythms and moods, knows what belongs and what is out of place. Just a mile south of downtown it is impossible for him to get such a feel; the hospitals alone throw it off, with strangers coming and going like so many transients. There are also plenty of actual transients.

Turning east on Pennsylvania he is in a canyon of hospitals and medical supply companies. There is no retail as far as the eye can see. *This new guy will never survive*, Sal thinks.

He notices the building before he sees the sign for the shop; it has been painted the most hideous lime green he has ever seen. Strike two.

The name, however, is no strike three: "The Globe Bookshop," with this motto etched on the front door: "Bringing you the world, one page at a time." Catchy. Sal swings his car into the lot beside the store. They have a decent-sized parking lot, a valuable commodity in any urban landscape.

He doesn't know what he expected to find upon entering the store, but it certainly wasn't this. While quite a bit smaller than The Last Word, The Globe Bookshop *feels* bigger inside. Rather than rows and rows of cases filling

52

the space, the bookcases only line the side walls of the long rectangular space. There are table displays running down the middle, broken up by strategically placed chairs and what looks like a booth from an old diner. Framed photographs of authors, both living and dead, adorn the tops of the bookcases. And in either a stroke of marketing genius or a lack of funds for sufficient inventory, on the shelves there as many books facing out as there are with only the spine visible; cover-out sells.

As he inspects a novel from Paraguay, a man emerges from the back room. Ben was right about one thing: this guy is no hipster (he'll have to just trust Ben on the obviously not gay part). He is around 50, with wild salt-and-pepper hair and a white beard. The jeans, cowboy boots, and Gin Blossoms T-Shirt may be what Ben is basing his assessment on. He moves toward the man, extending his hand.

"I'm – "

"Sal Terranova," the man says; his grip is firm. "Like I wouldn't know who you are."

"Crime TV?" Sal asks defensively.

"Shelf Awareness," he replies, naming an online magazine dealing solely with the book trade. "I'm Paco."

"I'm surprised that I didn't hear about you until today," Sal says, following him back to the front counter.

"I'm not," Paco answers. "Not really. We kind of live in different worlds."

"Different worlds? We're maybe three miles apart, if that."

"Yeah, but there's a world of difference between downtown and where you're standing now. And we're in different worlds in many other ways."

"How so?" Sal asks, suddenly not liking the guy's tone.

"For example, you own your building, right? The one that houses both the bookstore and your apartment?"

"Yes."

"That's two major expenses you don't have that I do," Paco says. "Worlds apart from the start."

"You're a grumpy bastard," Sal says. "Please continue."

"If you insist. You are in a virtual paradise there in downtown. For the most part the sidewalks are clean, safe, and full of foot traffic. Down here we're in something of a no-man's land; development is coming, new people are moving in, and in a couple of years this may be the new hot area. But we all have to survive until then."

"Which is why you envy my status as building owner as well as store owner," Sal says. It's a fair point.

"I envy your reputation too," Paco says. "Not your criminal one – yeah, I know about that too – but the history of your shop. The Last Word may be new, but your uncle's bookstore has been an institution downtown since I was a little kid. Here I'm starting from scratch, just trying to get our name out there any way possible."

Sal gazes around the store.

"Don't you think you're limiting yourself by carrying all these works in translation, classics, stuff like that. You don't even have a kids' section."

"There's a children's bookstore a few miles from here, on Montgomery," Paco says. "Why would I want to compete with another indie bookseller?"

"There's a store in Fort Worth that only sells children's books?" Sal asks.

Paco shakes his head and stares at Sal for a long moment before speaking.

"You really do live in a bubble, don't you?" he finally asks. "Yes, there is such a place. It's small, but extremely well run. You should get out more."

"Maybe so. So tell me about all these translations; do you sell many of them?"

"A fair amount, yeah," Paco says. "The idea of reading more than just the latest James Patterson ghost-written thriller or Nicholas Sparks fluff is starting to gain some traction. Reading authors from around the world expands your way of looking at things."

"I suppose so. But can you make a living with just that?"

"Time will tell," he says. "Doing alright so far."

"First year is the hardest," Sal says, though his first year really wasn't all that bad.

"That is what they say," Paco agrees.

The front bell chimes, loudly enough to wake the dead, and several people enter.

"I'll let you get back to it," Sal says. "It was good meeting you."

"You too," Paco answers. "Stop by any time, and feel free to buy a book next time."

Sal ignores this, but does have one last thought as he stops at the door.

"So there's a children's bookstore just down the road, huh?"

"Indeed," Paco says. "Yours, mine, hers, all within a mile or so radius. A couple more and we'd actually have a book town."

6

"Briarwood"

Jake wakes up Tuesday morning thinking he has had the strangest dream: an old lumberjack claiming to be the Apostle Paul showed up at his door and made him recite Bible verses from memory. He rubs his eyes and walks out to the kitchen to make coffee, but quickly realizes he can already smell coffee. The lumberjack from his dream, who was not a dream at all, has already made some.

"Oh my lord," he says, staring at Paul. "You're not a figment of my imagination."

"Of course I'm not, boy" Saul says. "Now let's go to that Catholic store."

"Not so fast old-timer," Jake says, pouring a cup of coffee for himself. "I have some things to do this morning, and you really can't come with me.

"That's fine," he says. "I can read until you get back."

Jake hesitates, causing the old man to arch one bushy eyebrow.

"You can't be worried that I'm a lunatic intent on robbing you," he says with a chuckle. "If that were the case your stuff would be gone already."

Jake cannot find a good argument against this, though he is not completely reassured.

"Ok," he says. "I won't be gone long. Do not answer the phone or the door until I get back."

Jake returns home from a meeting with several other church outreach leaders three hours later. As he opens the door he hears the raised voices of two men. One voice is Saul's; he can hear him clearly. The other man's voice is more muffled. He rushes to the living room to find Saul engaged in a heated debate…with a TV preacher on one of the Christian cable channels. It is all he can do to not burst out laughing. Saul hears him enter and turns, his face crimson.

"Do you know what this charlatan is preaching?" he demands.

Jake looks past him at the screen. The man on the television is Joel Swindon, a pastor in Houston with a congregation nearly as large as Briarwood's. His suit probably cost as much as Jake's entire wardrobe and his perfectly styled hair could have withstood hurricane-force winds. He called himself a pastor, but in reality he is a televangelist, a huckster, a shill.

"I know him," Jake says. "Everyone knows him. His last book was a bestseller for 36 weeks."

"I'm not surprised," Saul says indignantly. "With that slick smile he could sell sand to a Bedouin."

"He preaches what's called a "prosperity gospel," Jake explains. "Basically the idea is that God wants everyone to be fabulously wealthy, successful, and happy all the time, and all you have to do for that to happen is have enough faith."

"Have faith and give this guy a huge portion of their money," Saul says. "No suffering if you have enough faith? Has he ever heard of Job? Has he ever heard of *me*?"

"It's crazy, I know. But people want an easy road."

"And if you're poor or suffering it means you lack faith," he goes on. "Sounds like the Hindu caste system to me."

"You met Hindus in your travels?" Jake asks, surprised.

"A few," he says, "but I was talking about ones I know now."

Jake is stunned by this, and Saul can tell.

"Does it surprise you that there would be Hindus in heaven?" he asks with a smile. "Then brace yourself: there are Muslims and Buddhists too, and more than a few Baptists who were shocked that they didn't make it in."

Jake starts to ask more, but happens to glance at his watch; he is on a tight schedule.

"I want to talk more about this," he says, "but we need to head over to the church so I can pick up those commentaries for you. The set I have here is more for sermon preparation, but there is one in my office that's more explanatory. You should start with those. We can also pick you up some clothes while we're there."

"Clothes?" Saul asks.

"I noticed that you don't have a bag or anything with you, just what you're wearing. We have a food pantry and clothes closet at the church, and I can grab some clothes for you there."

"That's very kind of you," he says, the starts to pull on his boots. He looks back at the television when he's done.

"I certainly hope your sermons aren't like his," he says. "My mission is hard enough as it is."

"What mission?" Jake asks. He had not mentioned anything about a mission.

"I will explain everything soon. For now, let me get accustomed to this very different world I find myself in."

Jake wonders if he means the world of the 21st century or the world outside his mental institution. He has done some checking, and found no one matching Saul's description missing from any of the local hospitals or psych wards. This proves nothing, of course, but he had hoped the answer might be a simple one. The answer is never simple.

As they drive onto the campus of Briarwood Baptist Church in far north Fort Worth, Jake hears a sharp intake of breath from Saul, which is a common reaction when seeing the place for the first time. Briarwood is no small, quaint, A-Frame church building like you see on Christmas cards. In fact, several times it had been mistaken by tourists for the Alliance Mall that was located a few miles west of the campus. And while in most cases it might be more appropriate to say they drove onto the church "property," in reality "campus" is a more accurate word. Briarwood is actually bigger than the local Community College, situated on 130 acres of some of the most expensive land in the state.

Jake pulls into his reserved parking spot and kills the engine, but he doesn't get out immediately. There is a small sign inserted into the grass where the asphalt of the lot stops:

RESERVED FOR REV. JAKE DONOVAN
MINISTER OF OUTREACH AND EVANGELISM

"What are we waiting for?" Saul asks.

"Sorry," Jake says. "Force of habit. I always sit and stare at that sign for a minute or two. Part of me still can't believe that's my name on the sign."

"Ah, the sweet sin of pride," Saul says with a wry laugh.

He gets out of the truck before Jake can respond, but in spite of his jibe, one thing is certain: Briarwood Baptist Church is amazing to behold, a place that none of the first century saints could have ever imagined as they were meeting in houses, catacombs, and along the banks of rivers.

One of the new breed of mega-churches, it needed every one of those 130 acres of prime real estate. The sanctuary seats 10,000 at one time, and has theater-seating, huge video screens, and a sound system that rivals the Bass Performance Hall in downtown Fort Worth. In fact, the church often hosted concerts by popular Christian bands as well as conferences simulcast around the world. To the east of this main building there was a smaller chapel which seated only 800 people; it was reserved for weddings and more intimate gatherings.

As awe-inspiring as the sanctuary and chapel are, the rest of the complex is equally impressive. As they walk through the main entrance, they face a library and a bookstore; to their right down a long ramp is a fully staffed cafeteria, beyond which lay the offices of the ministerial staff. To the left is the food court, consisting of two fast-food chain restaurants and a coffee bar, flanked by a two-screen movie theater. A plethora of meeting rooms branch off the hallway that circles the entire second floor of the building and looks down on an atrium with trees and a fountain that sprays jets of water almost to the ceiling.

Connected to this building by an enclosed walkway is the children's building, where the offspring of church members could roam, romp, and learn about the Lord in comfort and safety while their parents did the same in the "big church." Briarwood took the safety of their little ones as seriously as their spiritual instruction: every parent had a photo ID badge that matched a corresponding sticker placed on each child while on campus, and this badge had to be shown to pass through the only entrance to the children's area. This entrance was guarded at all times by off-duty police officers who were also members.

Saul gives Jake a skeptical look as he tells him this.

"So if you don't have the badge you can't get your child back?" he asks.

"You can," Jake says, "but it's no simple process, especially with the infants who can't simply identify someone as mom or dad. And the officers take their duties very seriously. One Sunday they kept me out because I didn't have my staff badge with me."

"But they know who you are," he says. "You are basically one of their bosses on Sunday."

"All the more reason to follow procedures to the letter," Jake says. "The parents who were there thought it was hilarious."

To the west of the main building is a fairly recent addition: Briarwood Christian Academy. BCA is a fully-accredited school for grades K through 12, and even though it accommodates over one thousand students, twice that many were on the waiting list to get in. Beyond the school building is another two-story structure which holds a ten-lane bowling alley, gym, and an Olympic-sized pool; past that building are softball and soccer fields, and an impressive football stadium. The older deacons had drawn the line at putting a dome on the stadium: too flashy, they said.

The final building Jake points out to him lies even beyond the football field and can barely be seen from where they stand. It looks oddly out of place, a small two-story townhouse in the middle of a field with a short driveway connecting it to the road that circles the property. There were plans to add several more in the near future, but for now it stands alone.

"That's the missionary house," Jake says. "We let overseas missionaries who are back in the States for a while...we call it furlough...stay there."

"I certainly qualify as a missionary," Saul says.

"I may be able to get you set up there in a week or so, unless God or men in white coats take you away before then."

"Such unbelief from one who claims to be a believer," he says. His tone is not light, and while Jake had been joking clearly he is not.

"Hey," Jake says. "Learn to take a joke."

"I don't think you were joking," he says, "at least about the men in white coats. I can only assume what that means, and it can't reflect well on my sanity."

"You have to admit your story is hard to believe," Jake says, more defensively than he intends.

"It's funny," Saul says stopping and looking hard at him. "You believe that God would have a fish swallow

Jonah to get his attention, but not that he could send me to get yours."

Jake has no answer to that, and they walk on in silence until they enter the main building again.

"This complex epitomizes current Christian thought on how the spiritual life should be lived," he says to Saul as they walk toward his office. "'Stay unpolluted by the world. Everything you need is here.'"

"More like 'climb the stairway to heaven and then pull the ladder up after you as fast as you can'" he mutters, but Jake ignores him.

They pass through the outer waiting area where Jake's secretary, shared with the Minister of Music, usually acts as personal organizer and guard dog, and into his office. If Saul thought the reserved parking sign was a source of unhealthy pride for Jake, he definitely will not tell him how he feels about this office. It is, in a word, gorgeous/amazing/stupendous/wonderful. Actually, it can't be kept to just one word.

The carpet is walnut colored and luxuriantly thick (Jake often took his shoes and socks off and walked across it barefoot). One wall holds built-in floor-to-ceiling bookcases and another, also floor-to-ceiling, is all glass, a huge window looking out over an undeveloped part of the property. The wall behind his mahogany desk and leather chair hold his degrees from Baylor and the Seminary as well as numerous other honors.

His desk, which is big enough for an F-16 to land on, is clear except for two photographs: one of Jake, Ortiz, and a young woman taken many years ago and another of Jake and General Colin Powell. In his defense, his desk is much smaller than the Senior Pastor's.

Saul sinks down into one of the overstuffed chairs that flank a small circular table, and watches Jake intently.

"What?" he asks.

"What are you thinking about?" he asks. "You had a faraway look in your eyes."

"I was just remembering the first office I had when I entered the ministry," he says. "It was the trunk of my car."

"So on the whole you'd rather be here," he says.

"Of course," he says, with more conviction than he feels. He turns to his bookshelves. "So do you only want the commentaries on your letters, or should we bring the Gospels and Acts as well?"

"Might as well bring all of it," he says. "I'm a fast reader. And I would really love to see how you translated Luke's accounts of my travels. That is one I know very well, having read the final draft before he sent it out to everyone."

Jake looks around the office for a box, but cannot find one. He walks out to the copier that stands near his secretary's desk; there is a half-empty box of copier paper beside it. Jake loads the paper into the copier (she would have been quite unhappy if he had just stacked it on the floor) and takes the box back to his office. He loads the books into it and they head over to the sports building, which is where they stored food and clothing that was distributed to those in need.

With a church the size of Briarwood it isn't hard to fill several rooms with clothing people no longer wanted. Food was another matter, and every year Jake had to make several appeals as their stocks dwindled, especially during the summer; people just didn't get that hunger doesn't only strike the poor and homeless between Thanksgiving and Christmas. In less than fifteen minutes they find enough jeans, shirts, slacks, and other items to comfortably outfit Saul, all neatly packed into a large suitcase someone donated. It is only then that Jake realizes he will have to take him to the store for more basic things like underwear, socks, and toiletries. If he was overwhelmed by Damascus Road Bookstore, Wal-Mart might just kill him. Maybe he would just get the stuff for him.

As they drive through the parking lot, having loaded everything into the back of the truck, Saul glances back at the cluster of buildings.

"I would like to see what a worship service here looks like," he says. "Can I come with you on Sunday?"

"Of course," Jake says, though if by some miracle Saul is who he says he is, Jake is glad he's not preaching this weekend. Preaching in front of the Apostle Paul would bring a level of nervousness he had never experienced before.

7

"Story Time with Uncle Sal"

The store is filled to capacity with moms and small children for story time in the children's section. This weekly event was thrust upon Sal one day while all of the female staff were at a spa "bonding," and while he was angry about it at first, he had quickly found himself enjoying it. He continued to do the readings himself, even when Julia and Heather had volunteered to take over. But today he is nowhere to be seen.

"Where is he?" Camden demands through clenched teeth. Julia can merely shrug; she has no clue.

The children are on the verge of rioting now, some crying, some wailing, all chanting "Uncle Sal!" at the top of their pint-sized lungs. Heather is looking for an exit out of the sea of miniature humanity, though whether she could reach the door without the frustrated moms beating her to death with sippy cups is uncertain. She had tried to step in and start the story, but the little monsters had shouted her down.

Just when it seems the entire scene is about to tip into the abyss, the front door flies open and a tall figure in a black cape and absurdly tall top hat charges into the scrum. The children part like the Red Sea and fall silent as the new arrival removes his hat and bows to the crowd.

"Uncle Sal!" the children scream in unison as they begin jumping up and down happily.

The mothers visibly relax, and Heather breathes for the first time in what feels like hours. Sal swipes the book she is holding from her hand and glares at it disapprovingly.

"*Illustrated Classics for Children?*" he scoffs as he tosses the book to the side, causing the kids to giggle with glee.

"That is a fine book," Heather retorts. "You have no room to criticize. Last week you read them a story about a gangster from *A History of the New York Mob.*"

Sal stares at her open-mouthed and wide-eyed, making the kids laugh even harder. "Lucky Luciano is not a gangster. Who is Mr. Lucky, kids?"

"A magical Italian prince!" they reply.

"Indeed," Sal says, a satisfied grin spreading across his face.

"I cannot believe —" Heather begins, but Sal cuts her off.

"Kids," he says, "if we give Miss Heather a book…"

"She's going to say it's not as good as Hemingway!" they all scream together. All the moms are laughing now.

"Exactly." Sal winks at Heather, or rather at her back, for she is already stalking away, muttering curses.

"I am sorry I was delayed, my friends," he says to the children as he sits down in a large leather armchair he has procured specifically for this weekly event, "but I could not find my cape. And it's not a proper story time without a cape, is it?"

The children shake their heads and then sit down as close to the big chair as possible. They gaze expectantly at Sal, waiting for the question that will determine who gets to sit on his lap while he reads.

"Today's question is a tough one," he warns them. They scrunch up their little faces in concentration. "There once was a drummer who only got to play on one song that Bruce Springsteen released. But that song was *Born to Run*. What was his name?"

There are shouts of "Max!" and "Vini!" and even one "Ringo," this last clearly from a newcomer to the group. In addition to stories Sal has been educating a new generation of Springsteen fans.

"No, no, I said only one song," Sal reminds them.

A toddler who can barely toddle leaps to his feet and rushes straight at Sal. He grabs Sal around the calf, looks up at him and yells: "Boom!" Sal stares at the youngster in amazement.

"That is correct young man!" he shouts over the din. "Ernest 'Boom' Carter only played on one song in his E-Street Band career, but what a song it was. Well done!"

He hoists the happy child, who likely only knows a few words – "boom" being one of them – onto his lap and opens the story they always begin with: *If You Give a Mouse a Cookie*. The room immediately falls silent.

"I'll say this for my cousin," Camden whispers to Julia. "He has a way with kids."

Julia doesn't answer, and when Camden turns to look at her she immediately recognizes the expression on her face.

"Oh good lord," she continues. "You've decided you want to have babies with him."

"I decided that a long time ago," Julia replies without taking her eyes off Sal. "Times like this only prove that I'm right about it."

"You realize that on any given day he's as likely to rob a jewelry store as sell a book?"

Julia shakes her head and smiles.

"Not a chance," she replies. "Like you said, the key is to keep him occupied with some crazy quest, like the book town thing he mentioned to me last night. Sal loves tilting at windmills."

"Well I hope you can keep him on the straight and narrow, Dulcinea," Camden says. Julia stares at her, astonished.

"What?" Camden asks. "I read *Don Quixote* in school. I'm not nearly as illiterate of some of you seem to think."

8

"What's in a Name?"

Back at Jake's apartment they spend some time getting Saul settled into the guest room. It should suit his needs perfectly; since Jake's few guests are usually visiting preachers the room has a desk and computer in it as well as the normal bedroom setup. They unpack the clothes into a dresser and stack Jake's commentaries on the small shelf beside the desk.

"Do you realize that this room is bigger than most of the houses I stayed in back in the old days?" he asks. Jake's knowledge of the history of that time is pretty good, and he assures Saul that he is aware of this fact.

It takes considerably longer than Jake expects to show him how to work the computer, and in hindsight he's not sure why he shows him at all. But he eventually gets the basic idea of it, and Jake leaves him alone to read while he runs to the store to get the rest of Saul's essential clothing and personal hygiene items.

When he returns an hour later, Saul has his head stuck in the fridge, and Jake startles him when he says his name.

"Don't sneak up on me like that, boy," he says. "Do you have any chili? I had the television on while I read through the commentary on Galatians…that guy had some good points but missed a lot of my meaning…and a man dressed in a funny hat asked how long it's been since I had a steaming bowl of Wolf Brand Chili. Well, I've never had one, so I thought I'd try it."

Jake laughs and opens the pantry door, and to his surprise he actually does have a few cans of Wolf Brand. He empties one into a pan and puts it on the stove to heat. Then he gets out some Fritos and shredded cheese.

"Frito pie," he tells Saul. "The best way to eat chili."

While they eat they discuss the plan for tomorrow. Jake has meetings all morning, but will be able to come get him for lunch. He says that is fine; he would be deep in study anyway.

"I suppose you have decided I am not a lunatic," he says as he scrapes the bottom of his bowl.

"What makes you say that?" Jake asks. "I haven't decided yet."

"Do you normally leave lunatics alone in your house while you go to work?"

"Not normally, no," he admits.

"Sounds like a decision to me," he says. Then he gets up and goes back to his room.

Jake looks at his watch; it's time for him to meet Heather for coffee. He grabs his keys and walks to the guest room, knocks, and opens the door a crack.

"I won't be long," Jake says through the door.

"Tell the young lady hello for me," Saul replies.

The Daily Grind is almost empty when Jake and Heather enter: the after-work crowd won't show up for a few more hours. They order and then find a seat near the back on an overstuffed couch.

"Are you sure you wouldn't rather go to a restaurant?" Jake asks.

"Nope," Heather replies. "Food would just make me sleepy; I need the extra caffeine to get me through to closing time."

He nods, then spends some time closely examining a frayed patch on their couch. After a few minutes of this, Heather can take no more.

"What's wrong?" she asks.

Jake looks up, still unsure whether he should tell her. He decides he should.

"I have a confession," he says, not meeting her eyes.

Her shoulders slump.

"You're gay and in love with Ortiz," she says before he can continue. "I knew it; all the good ones are gay."

Jake is so stunned he momentarily can't form words.

I am not gay," he finally says. "And I am definitely not in love with Ortiz."

"Then you're back with the blonde Amazon who came to the bookstore with you the first time we met."

"Good lord, no," he says. "Being in love with Lou would be better than that."

"Then what else can there be to confess?" she asks, eyeing him warily. "On the run from the law? Three wives in three different states? A secret love for the music of Barry Manilow? What?"

"Saul isn't really my uncle," he says.

"Oh." She certainly had not expected this. This is no big deal. "Who is he then? And why would you say he's your uncle if he's not?"

Now the hard part.

"Well, he is actually, or at least actually claims to be, the Apostle Paul."

She laughs, but quickly stops when she sees he is not laughing.

"Seriously?" she asks, as incredulous as you would expect from a normal, rational person. "He seriously thinks he's the Apostle Paul? *You* seriously think he's the Apostle Paul?"

"I still have a few doubts, obviously," he admits, trying his best not to sound defensive. "I am starting to wonder though."

"How? How can you even wonder? When some stranger tells you he's the reincarnation of the guy who wrote half the New Testament you don't wonder; you call the Psych Ward."

"He's not the reincarnation of Paul," Jake corrects her. "He's the actual guy. Come back from heaven, or wherever."

"That makes even less sense," she says. "I could almost believe a reincarnation story."

Jake finds this quite odd, but lets it pass.

"He knows things about me that no one could possibly know," Jake says, staring into his cup rather than looking at her.

"You can find out all sorts of things online, Jake," she replies.

"Not these things," he says. "He knows things I've *dreamed*."

She ponders this for a moment, then smiles.

"Maybe he's a psychic," she says. "That would explain it."

"So you can believe he's a psychic who can see into my dreams, but not the Apostle Paul."

"Being a psychic is way more believable," she replies confidently. "I know lots of psychics, but no Texas-visiting saints." She is not kidding.

"Right," Jake says, since he can think of no other response. "Anyway, I wanted to tell you even though you might decide I'm as crazy as, well, as he might be."

"Nothing wrong with a little lunacy," she says, wiping some foam from the latte from her upper lip. "And the old guy seems harmless enough. But it's going to take a lot more than a little mind-reading to convince me that he's some heavenly messenger."

"Like what, for example?"

"I don't know," she replies. "Like turning coffee into wine or turning Sal into a pillar of salt or something."

"That would convince you, huh?" he asks, not even attempting to hide his laughter.

"That would do it."

When Jake gets home, Saul is sitting at the kitchen table drinking coffee and reading from the commentary on the Book of Acts, his new Bible open beside it. He looks up, nods, and goes back to reading.

Not wanting to interrupt, Jake grabs a bottle of water from the fridge; he has had enough coffee for one night.

"Maybe you should take a break," he says. "All work and no play makes Paul a dull boy."

"Saul," he says.

Jake stares at him for a minute, trying to decide if he should ask a question that has been on his mind since they met. He decides to go ahead and ask, since the guy could be gone at any time and the opportunity would be lost.

"You keep telling me to call you Saul," he says after taking a drink of water, "but God changed your name to Paul after your conversion."

"Did not," he says.

"Did too," Jake insists. "Luke even wrote down when it happened."

"Go back and look again. It says 'Saul, who was also called Paul.' Not changed, just switched to the Latinized version to fit in as I worked among the Gentiles of the Empire."

"I don't think that's right," Jake says firmly, not quite knowing why this is such an important point.

"Hey, I should know. You think Peter called me Paul? Well he did, actually, but not in Judea. There I was always Saul."

"That makes no sense."

He does one of those arched eyebrow things again. He would have made a great movie villain if he hadn't been a saint and dead for 2,000 years. Those were two big obstacles to a career in film.

"Tell me," he says. "If you lived in Spain, what would they call you?"

"They'd call me Jake," Jake says, not sure where he's going with this.

"That's not your given name," Saul says.

"Okay, maybe they would call me John. But I wouldn't like it."

"You think?" he persists. "Everybody?"

Jake thinks hard for a minute, and then it dawns on him.

"Well, I suppose some would call me Juan."

"Right. Same thing. And I have an even better example, using a contemporary of yours I just read about on that Internets thing"

"Internet," Jake corrects him. "No *s*."

"Whatever. Anyway, this guy also happens to have my name. When Saul Hudson is at home for Passover, do you think his mother calls him by the name she gave him at birth, which was Saul?"

"I don't know who that is," Jake says, "but I suppose she would."

"Ah, but you do know him. And you would not call him Saul."

"What would I call him then?"

"You would call him Slash," he says with a huge grin. "He was the guitarist for Guns 'N Roses. Two names, two contexts, same guy."

Nice, Jake thinks. The greatest theologian in history knows about Guns 'N Roses. Was there a special place in Hell for corrupting a saint?

"I listened to some of their songs; they were pretty good," he continues. "There was 'Sweet Child O Mine,' 'Patience,' and 'November Rain.'"

"Yeah, well let's keep you away from 'One in a Million' and 'Rocket Queen.' Next you'll want a guitar."

"No way, son," he replies "Even in my day it was the drummers who got the girls."

Jake can't tell if he's joking, and is frankly afraid to ask. So he simply nods and moves to the couch. Saul goes back to reading the commentary, and just before Jake turns on the television he can hear him humming the guitar solo from "Sweet Child O Mine."

9

"What's So Funny About Peace, Love, and
Divination?"

Sal knows trouble when he sees it, and a petite blonde with
a ponytail and a yoga mat slung across her back is always
trouble. He hopes that she will veer off toward their
admittedly tiny New Age section, but fortune does not
smile on him this day: she is making a beeline straight for
him.

"Hi," she says, much too brightly for him this early in
the morning, but then she has probably been up for hours,
having already eaten a bowl of gluten-free, vegan tree bark
and aligned her chakras with an hour of downward-facing,
tree-climbing, howler monkey poses. He grunts a greeting.

"I'm Amber," she continues, unfazed by his lack of
returned sunshine. "I want to discuss a business proposal
with the owner."

"That would be me," he replies, "but I'm really busy right now."

She looks around the empty store, clearly confused. She decides to press on.

"I'll make it quick," she says. "I'd like to use part of the store for a class." She pauses, thinking hard; class is not the word she wants. He watches as the wheels spin, gaining no traction for some time. "Not a class exactly." More spinning. "What I need is a good public space to set up a small table to do Tarot readings." She beams at him, proud to have found the right words.

He does not beam back. In fact, he's not sure he's heard her correctly, as he is still two cups of coffee short of human.

"Tarot readings," he finally repeats. "You want to tell people's fortunes in my shop?"

The beam vanishes instantly, replaced by a look of horror.

"It is not fortune telling," she replies. Her voice has not changed in tone or volume, though her eyes convey her alarm. "It is revealing for people the path that lies ahead for them, or that may lie ahead depending on their choices."

"Ah. So it's basically not much of anything then."

"It is *guidance*," she insists, eyes narrowing, tone unchanged. "It is comforting to have some light on the path ahead in order to stumble less."

It is entirely too early for this nonsense.

"And you want to perform this illumination here why exactly?"

"All the time slots at the yoga studio are filled for months in advance," she explains. "I'm just a new yogi, and I get last choice on everything until I advance more." He tries, with a fair amount of success, not to laugh that she called herself a yogi. "I asked Paco at The Globe Bookshop first," she continues, "but he said that his store had been an illegal gambling den and brothel in the 1930s and the uncleansed negative energy would interfere with my readings. He suggested I come see you."

The grumpy old bastard, Sal thinks. *He will pay for this.*

"We have a similar problem here," he answers, thinking quickly. "This building faces northeast, which aligns it with the Meridian of Odin. The Norse energy is very violent at times, and would surely skew your readings. The results could be disastrous."

Amber's face clouds; she grasps the words "meridian" and "Odin" and "Norse," but her training is all Hindu-centric. Not wanting to appear ignorant, she simply nods.

"That would be bad," she agrees.

"But I tell you what," Sal says, doing his best to appear helpful. "Crain Rare Books on 5th Street has a statue of Ganesh on one of their shelves (it's true; Randal likes elephants) and I bet he would be glad to let you set up there."

The brilliant smile returns, and Amber pivots immediately and heads toward the door. Before she reaches it, Sal calls out a question.

"Do you charge for these readings?" he asks.

"Yes," she answers, only half-turning back to him and not breaking stride. "But I'm a novice, so I only get $75 for a 30-minute session." The word session is abruptly cut off by the closing door, but all Sal hears is $75 for 30 minutes of talking shit. Hell, he does that every day for free. And an idea begins to form.

The following afternoon Julia walks into the back room to find Sal hunched over a table, meticulously affixing something to a rectangle of poster board slightly larger than the size of a playing card. A stack of similar blank cards sits to one side of the table, along with an X-Acto knife, glue, another stack of papers roughly the same size as the cut-out poster board, and a small jar of silver paint with a brush sticking out of it. Scrap poster board, paper, tape, and other detritus litter the floor at his feet.

"What in the world are you doing?" she asks, fairly certain she won't like the answer.

"Working on an alternate stream of revenue," he says. "Hand me that tray over there." He points to the counter beside the sink.

She moves past him to the counter and picks up the tray. It is covered with the rectangular shapes, all painted silver. She sets the tray down on the table and takes a seat next to him. Sal lightly touches one of the cards with his pinky finger; seeing that the paint is dry he flips the cards, ten in all, over.

Julia has no clue what she is seeing. At first glance they appear to be nothing more than homemade playing cards. On closer inspection, however, this is clearly not the case. There are numbers on some of the cards, but not in the normal place, and there are no hearts, spades, clubs, or diamonds. The face cards – they all seem to be face cards, in fact – are also not kings, queens, or jacks. Each face is different, and after a brief moment she recognizes all of them: Hemingway, Dickens, Steinbeck, Atwood, Bronte (Charlotte or Emily, she always confuses them), even Stephen King.

"What -?" she says, turning to face him.

"Literary tarot cards, my dear Julia," he says with a wicked smile that worries her even more. "An idea brought on by a fortuitous visit from a yogi who was neither a bear nor a Yankees catcher."

"You're going to need to elaborate on that just a bit," she replies.

Sal tells her the story of the novice yoga fortune teller.

"I still don't get it," she says. "What does that nonsense have to do with all this…nonsense?"

"I have decided to enter into the ancient art of divination," Sal replies. "But I want my cards to be more literary – and cooler – than the ones we can order from our vendors. Did you know we can order tarot decks from our vendors? I didn't. Anyway, I have created my own deck, or almost finished creating it. What do you think?"

"I don't really understand what it's supposed to look like," she says, examining the Stephen King card; it has the word "DEATH" written at the bottom. "The pictures are nice, and I like the silver on the back side."

"It was on sale," he interrupts. "It's called Silver Bullet."

"Right. But what are they supposed to represent?"

"Stephen King is, of course, Death. Hemingway is the Magician. Faulkner is the Fool."

"I don't know why you hate him so much. He wrote some very good books, and his speech accepting the Nobel Prize was amazing."

"Hemingway hated him," Sal says flatly. "So, I hate him. Heather agrees."

"And what do you plan to do with all of this once you're done?" She already knows that she, and certainly Camden, will not like the answer.

"I will tell people their future, their path, their whatever. I will be Swami Sal."

"Oh my lord. And how much will you charge for this glimpse into the future?"

"Fifty bucks for a 30-minute session," he says, gluing a picture of Oscar Wilde onto a blank card. "Have to undercut the competition."

Sal sits at a small table in Jacob's rare book room several days later, facing an earnest young woman desperately seeking to know if she should leave her job as a corporate accountant to write romance novels full-time. He has had several of these writing or book-related clients since he put out word of his new service, which suits him just fine. Much better than a sixty-year-old lady wanting to know if her husband is sleeping with his twenty-five-year-old admin, or an old man wondering if the doctors are right. He won't take those clients; his hypocrisy has limits.

Finding a space to do the readings was easier than he had expected. He could have forced Jacob to let him use the room for an hour a day – two sessions – but an offer of twenty percent of the fee was enough to gain his complete cooperation. $100 a week that his wife wouldn't know about was too good to turn down.

The young woman gazes expectantly at Sal as he lays out the cards in a pattern roughly resembling the outline of an open book, one that is certainly not found in any tarot guide. He scrutinizes the upturned cards for a while, then speaks.

"It appears," he says in as soothing a tone as he can manage, "that you are meant to keep your current position for now. The Kerouac card normally indicates reckless abandon, but in this case it is inverted. Furthermore, the Dickens card trumps it, and Dickens was not only a great writer, but also a pragmatic businessman who supported two separate families. This tells me that while you should keep writing, your first duty is to your family, and that your current job as an insurance claims processor does that, while writing alone might not. We can read the cards again in six months or a year, after you've actually written a novel, and see if this has changed."

The woman nods, seemingly relieved, hands him two twenties and a ten, and gets up from the table. On the way out she buys the latest "You Can Write That Novel" guide. Once she is gone Sal hands the ten to Jacob; he pockets it without a word.

Julia and Camden are at the front counter, and after the woman has gone Julia turns to Camden.

"I'm surprised you're allowing this," she says. "Normally you find a way to shut down his crazier schemes."

"Just wait," she replies, eyeing the front door. "This particular scheme ends today."

At that moment, the door opens and Jake enters with Ortiz. Julia glances at Camden, who shakes her head. The door immediately opens again, and the one person in all of Texas that Sal fears rushes inside: Sister Mary Louise, the mystery novel-loving nun from St. Joseph's Cathedral down the block. She flies past Jake and Ortiz, scanning the room for Sal. Camden expects him to flee out the back, but to her surprise he does not.

"Salvatore Terranova!" the nun screams, "What is this I hear about you practicing witchcraft? And for money, no less!"

Sal smiles – actually smiles – and both Camden and the nun are momentarily taken aback. He gestures for them to follow him into the rare book room, and all of them, including Jake and Ortiz, do so. Several bewildered customers simply stare after them.

"I've been expecting you, sister," Sal says, much more calmly than he has ever spoken to her before.

"How?" she demands. "Did you read it in your little deck of Lucifer cards?"

Jake laughs, but a withering glance from Sister Mary Louise silences him.

"No," Sal replies. "I know because my cousin is maddeningly predictable. This time, however, she has overplayed her hand. No pun intended."

"You will stop this blasphemy at once, Salvatore," the nun says sternly, clearly expecting this proclamation to be sufficient.

"No," he replies, still smiling.

The room is stunned. Even Jacob, who wasn't really paying attention, now gapes at Sal in disbelief. The nun's face is turning a shade of crimson not typically seen on humans, but before she can erupt Sal continues.

"It's not divination or witchcraft, sister," he says in the same soothing tone he used with the client earlier. "It's also not blasphemous or Satanic or even, God forbid, Protestant." In spite of herself, the sister cracks a smile at this. "It is a combination of entertainment and coaching, and that's how I advertise it. There are no arcane or esoteric rituals involved, because I adapted the entire process to fit my style."

"That means he didn't study anything about actual tarot and just borrowed what he's seen on television or in a bar or someplace," Julia translates.

"And yet people enjoy coming because it's not only instructive, it's *fun*," he says. "Not evil, not anti-God – fun. Satan is not going to jump out of a card and drag anyone to Hell. My clients learn a little about famous authors, and a little about themselves. And then I get paid. It's a win-win-win."

"But –" the nun tries to respond, but Sal cuts her off again.

"And because I knew that Camden would get you involved at some point, I made a deck specially for you."

He removes a small package from a black pouch made of silk and places it on the table. The nun warily moves closer to the table to inspect it as he unwraps it. In perhaps the most amazing act of the day, Sal pulls a chair closer to him and motions for her to sit.

"You have Bingo Night at the cathedral annex once a month, right?" he asks once she is seated.

"Actually, twice a month now," she replies. "Money has been tight, so…"

"And you don't consider Bingo to be dangerous gambling. Same with raffles, church carnivals with games of chance, etc. This deck could be an addition to the entertaining activities that bring in a small amount for your many charitable activities."

This deck of cards is not filled with authors, but rather with saints. In fact, Sal has simply pasted saint cards he bought at St. Iraneus Bookstore onto slightly larger poster board cards and made the back side a uniform design: the Papal seal.

"Saints' cards?" the nun asks, though not in an accusatory way. "Surely that would be blasphemous?" It is a question, not a declaration.

"Sister," he says, "at St. Iraneus Bookstore they sell little statues of St. Joseph you can bury in your yard to help your house sell faster. This is clearly no more blasphemous than that."

"Point taken," she says. "But how would it work for one of your readings?" There is still a hint of distaste when she says the word *readings*.

"First of all, it won't be my reading, and I suggest it not be yours either. Get one of the Knights of Columbus or a CYO leader to do it. That way it doesn't look like the Church endorses it."

She nods. "Good idea."

Then," he continues, "it's simply a fun game with some implied guidance."

"Implied guidance?" Julia repeats.

"Yeah. With these cards the method and explanations are already set, some for thousands of years in fact. If, for example, you turn a St. Anthony card, the explanation is that something lost will be found. Never be too specific, no matter how much the person presses you. Vagueness is the key."

"You don't have any of the Trinity or the Blessed Virgin on any of these cards, do you Salvatore?" the nun asks.

"No. Even I know better than that. But we have to have the apostles."

"That's fine," she agrees. "And how much should we charge for a reading?"

"At a Bingo Night I would suggest a donation of ten to twenty dollars. Reasonable enough, and it won't make anyone scream to the Bishop if their 'fortune' doesn't come true."

"Ah, the Bishop," she says. "We want to keep him out of this for a totally different reason. He would surely want to keep the money for his grand plan."

"Grand plan?" Sal asks.

Sister Mary Louise sighs heavily before answering.

"The Bishop recently returned from a conference in Barcelona," she says. "While he was there, of course, he visited the Sagrada Familia Basilica."

"That's the one they've been building forever, right?" Camden asks. Ortiz smiles, pleased that she knows this.

The sister nods. "For more than 120 years. The famed architect Gaudi began the work in 1882. It's taken so long in part because construction only proceeds as they raise the necessary funds; no loans are ever taken. But even with that restriction it would have been completed decades ago if they didn't keep adding to the original plans. It is a marvelous building, but it has become a – what is the word?"

"Boondoggle," Jake says.

"Yes. A boondoggle."

"What does that have to do with the Bishop of Fort Worth?" Sal asks.

"The Bishop was so struck by the grandeur of the basilica that he decided to do the same thing at St. Joseph's. He wants to expand it indefinitely, as a visible sign of God's continuing work on earth."

"That's a little nuts," Sal says. "With all due respect to His Eminence."

"It is completely insane," the nun replies. "But apparently he is not the only insane Prince of the Church; he has received authorization from Rome to proceed, and even managed a clause in the official documents stating the work will continue even after his death or retirement."

"Ad infinitum," Luis says reverently.

"I don't understand how this impacts Bingo Night or the saint cards readings," Sal says. "Those are small-change events."

"No change is too small for his new mania," she says, a look of frustration creeping across her face. "In his 'wisdom' he has instituted a tithe on every dime that comes in through any channel related to the cathedral or the diocese."

"He's pulling ten percent of everything for the building fund?" Sal asks. The heads of the Five Families would be impressed.

"Indeed. Everything: the schools' tuition, all fundraisers, every offering taken up at Mass. It is going to put quite a strain on a lot of the parishes, but when the Pope gives his blessing you don't argue. I wouldn't even be considering this tarot/saint nonsense if we weren't in such need of cash."

"Give me some time to think this one through, sister," Sal says, looking at her with an expression that Julia recognizes, amazingly, as fondness. "It may be best if we take this, and some other things, underground."

"Underground?" the nun asks?

"Yes, away from the prying and well-meaning but clearly misguided eyes of the Bishop."

"That would be deceitful, Salvatore," she replies with little conviction.

"Not at all," he says. "It would be in the oldest and most revered traditions of the Church. When things got too hot for the first Christians, they fled to the catacombs to practice their faith without interference. You need to do the same, figuratively speaking."

"Perhaps," she says, rising to her feet. "I will discuss this with a few of the sisters at the convent – the more discreet ones – and get back with you."

When she is gone, Camden pulls Sal aside.

"I cannot believe you managed to get a nun to buy into this tarot thing," she says. "It's as crazy as the Bishop's perpetual building project."

"They're the same thing," Sal says with a smile. "In both cases, money makes the monkey dance."

10

"Nighttime Visitors"

While Saul pours over his commentaries, Jake spends the day checking hospitals, police stations, retirement homes, and mental health facilities, all in the hope of finding out who this guy really is. He has humored him up to this point, mainly because he is afraid the old gentleman might be a danger to himself or someone else if triggered somehow. Of course, there is the slightest of chances he could be who he says he is, but that is a leap too far for Jake's logical mind.

By 6:00 pm, Jake has confirmed that if Saul is indeed an escaped mental patient, it is from somewhere outside of the Dallas/Fort Worth, Austin, Houston, or San Antonio areas. He checked Oklahoma City and Tyler with no luck. He is also not on anyone's missing persons list. This doesn't prove or disprove anything, though; he could have wandered here from almost anywhere.

Saul emerges from his room, sits down on the couch and gives Jake a bemused smile.

"No luck finding which asylum I escaped from, I gather," he says. "You know Jake, I find your lack of faith disturbing."

"So you're an apostle *and* a Star Wars fan," Jake replies. Saul appears confused by this.

"I don't know what Star Wars is," he says, "but I still detect a sarcastic tone in your voice, I can see I will need help in convincing you."

"What kind of help?" Jake asks, not really paying attention. He is trying to decide if there is any way to do a nationwide search, some kind of escapee database or something.

"You will see," Saul says. "Tonight you will be visited by three visions."

"Three visions? Like the ghost of Christmas Past, Present, and Future in Dickens' *A Christmas Carol?*"

"I know who Dickens is," Saul replies. "I don't know anything about Christmas carols, except that they are festival songs of some kind. And I am not talking about ghosts, but rather…well, you'll see. Sleep well."

With that he gets up from the couch and returns to his room. When Jake walks to the door a few minutes later, the light is already off.

As he gets into bed several hours later, Jake is not worried about ghosts, which he doesn't believe in, or visions, which he never experiences. His mind at ease, he drifts off to sleep almost immediately.

Just after midnight Jake sits straight up in bed, awakened by the instinctive awareness that someone is standing at the foot of his bed. In his semi-conscious state he assumes it is an intruder and reaches under his pillow for the 9mm Beretta he always keeps there. Before he can take aim at the shape he remembers Saul; it's not an intruder, probably just the old guy wondering where something is.

He flips on the lamp on his nightstand and stares at the figure looming over him. It is definitely not Saul, but neither is it some garden-variety burglar. While not particularly tall or muscular, the man is the most imposing figure he has ever seen. He has long white hair and a long white beard, but is definitely no Santa Claus. He appears to be very old, at least 80, but a vibrant old, like Jack Palance before he died. He holds a thick wooden staff almost as tall as he is.

"John Kennedy Donovan," the man says. His voice is not spooky or ethereal, but firm and very human. "Your doubts about the Lord's servant Saul have come up before Him, and He is not pleased."

"Uh, right," Jake replies. "And who might you be, sir?"

"I am Moses. Like you, I tried to escape the Lord's call. But I did it by arguing my lack of ability."

Jake thought back to the account in the third chapter of Exodus, where God spoke to Moses through the burning bush. He told Moses to go and tell Pharaoh to free the Israelites from their bondage, but Moses did not want to go. Their back and forth takes up the entire fourth chapter of Exodus and in a nutshell goes something like this:

Moses: What if they don't believe me?

God: Toss your staff down and it will turn into a serpent. Then pick it up and it will turn into a staff again.

Moses: Yeah, that might do it. But you know, I'm no good at speaking to people. I stutter.

God: I will tell you what to say.

Moses: Look, this all cool and everything, but I'd really rather not go. Send somebody else.

God: Don't make me smite you; just do what I say.

"I don't see how your situation is even remotely similar to mine," Jake says, feeling a little foolish talking to what is clearly a dream. Yet not a dream…what did Saul say? 'You will be visited by three visions.'

"It is very similar," the vision of Moses replies. "I feared failure, ridicule, even death, and thus did not want to obey a very clear command from the Lord. You are no different. It is easier for you to believe my brother Saul is a madman, because if he is who he claims to be, you will be forced to make very hard, very uncomfortable choices,

choices that might change your life. And you do not like change."

"But God himself spoke to you," Jake protests. "It doesn't get much clearer than that. All I have is one old man claiming to be the Apostle Paul."

"He prefers Saul," Moses says.

"Sorry...Saul. But you see my point, right?"

"I do not see your point at all. God spoke to me through a burning bush; he is speaking to you through the return of one of his greatest servants. In essence they are the same thing."

"I'm not sure that's true," Jake says, with little conviction.

"Do not be stubborn," Moses replies. "It was that kind of attitude...and no small amount of misplaced anger, which you also have...that caused me to strike the rock when the Lord had instructed me only to speak to it. You know the result."

"You were not allowed to enter the Promised Land because of your disobedience," Jake says, suddenly feeling sorry for him. "But it did get you a mention in a Springsteen song," he adds under his breath.

"Do not let the same be said of you. It is a high price to pay."

With that, Moses vanishes. Jake can't sleep for some time after that, unless of course he has been sleeping the whole time and this is just one long dream. But eventually he drifts off again. At 2 a.m. he wakes suddenly with the same feeling he experienced before Moses appeared. This time he doesn't even bother to reach for his pistol. He simply flips on the light and stares at the man standing at the end of his bed, wondering who it is this time.

"John Kennedy Donovan," the man says. "Your doubts about the Lord's servant Saul have come up before Him, and He is not pleased."

"Someone pointed that out to me a couple hours ago," Jake replies, doing his best not to sound flippant. He certainly does not feel flippant. "Who are you, sir?"

His current visitor does not have the long hair and beard of his predecessor. His head is completely shaved, and his cheeks are smooth. He is rail-thin, but speaks with the authority of one used to making serious proclamations.

"I am Jonah," the man says. "I, too, ran from the Lord, just as you have been running."

"I have not been running," Jake says defensively. "I have been serving consistently for years." It sounds a little boastful even to him, but it's true.

"You did not try to take a ship to the opposite end of the world from where the Lord told you to go, this is true," the vision of Jonah agrees. "You have been running in a different, yet equally troubling manner."

"How is that?"

"That is for Saul to reveal," Jonah says, taking a seat on the edge of the bed. "Just know that in this you and I are more alike than you care to admit. I did not want to go to Nineveh because I was afraid of the Assyrians, who were mortal enemies of Israel. I had in my mind the way things should go, wanted God to do things my way. And when He did not I reacted like a petulant child."

"And that makes us alike how exactly?"

"Do not interrupt me!" Jonah exclaims, and his voice thunders through the room. "You think that you are following the Lord's leading, but you are really following your own. And all because you cannot release your anger, just like me and the vine."

Jake stares at him dumbfounded. He has just used the same condemnation against him, with a little paraphrasing, that God used against Jonah himself.

"That hurts," is all he can manage to say.

"And it should," Jonah says, his tone much kinder now. "It hurt me to hear it when the Lord said it to me. And my book ends with that condemnation, with no one ever knowing if I ever understood my errors. I did, and I pray that you will as well."

Before Jake can reply, Jonah is gone. The room is eerily silent, much more so than when Moses vanished. He ponders Jonah's words for what feels like a long time. What gifts was he talking about, and what anger? He's not angry about anything.

He is still turning these questions over in his mind, not ever falling asleep again, when the last of the promised three visitors appears. Though he does not know how, Jake immediately recognizes this man as the apostle Peter, the rock on whom Jesus said he would build His Church.

"John Kennedy Donovan," the man says. "Your doubts about the Lord's servant Paul have come up before Him, and He is not pleased."

"Wait," Jake says. "You called him Paul. He said you called him Saul."

"I called him Saul in Judea," the burly fisherman says impatiently. "Are we in Judea?"

"No," Jake answers sheepishly. "You are Peter, right?"

"Yes," Peter replies. "I am the final proof you will receive that Paul is who he claims to be, and that his message to you is from the Lord. Dismiss my warning at your peril."

"I suppose you're here to remind me that though you denied even knowing Jesus the night before his crucifixion, he restored you after you repented and you became the leader of the early church, just as he had said you would."

"You can suppose whatever you wish," Peter says sarcastically. "You would be wrong."

Jake sees that the Biblical description of Peter as a hothead had been accurate. He had better tread lightly or he might just receive a beating from this vision. Getting pummeled by a vision would be quite embarrassing; Luis would never let him live it down.

"I apologize for my presumption," he says. "What do you have to tell me?"

"I am here to address your, and my, greatest flaw," he says. "I suffered from, and you suffer from still, the sin of pride. It was I who proclaimed the loudest that I would never desert the Lord, I who reveled in my place as leader of the disciples before his resurrection, I who wanted to sit at his right hand."

Jake wants to interrupt, but knows better. He had made that mistake with Jonah, and he is fairly certain that Peter will not just bellow in response.

"You," Peter continues, "suffer from the same sort of pride. You love the trappings of your position at your new church, love people recognizing you, love being called the Defender of the Faith. You must come to the place, as I did, where you no longer seek to be the focal point, but rather one who does what needs doing without caring who gets the credit."

"You did that when you allowed Saul, I mean Paul, to ascend to the prominent place in the early church," Jake says.

"I did not allow it," Peter replies, "as it was not my choice to make. I accepted it as the plan the Lord had laid out before the creation of the world. I labored on, but in near obscurity, until my death. Which, by the way, you have all made far too much of; I was not worthy to be crucified in the same way as my Master, and so asked not to be. It did not make me heroic."

"Are you one of the ones visiting me because of your relationship with Paul?" Jake asks.

"Of course," Peter replies. "As I said in one of my letters, our dear brother Paul sometimes writes things that are hard to understand, but he is still my brother."

"So you're telling me that the man sleeping down the hall really is the apostle Paul?" Jake asks.

"In your heart, you knew the answer to that the day you met him. You are simply a stubborn man Jake Donovan, an attribute that I, of all people, can understand. Listen to him, and heed the word he brings you from the Lord. Few have been granted such a great honor."

And as quickly as he appeared, Peter is gone. His departure leaves Jake sad; Peter had always been his favorite apostle, and he had always seen past his flaws to the qualities Peter had as well. People focused on the fact that while he was walking on the water to Jesus, Peter saw the storm around him, was afraid, and began to sink; Jesus even asked him why he had so little faith. Yet Peter was the only one with the courage to get out of the damn boat in the first place.

And so, sometime between Peter's departure and the rising of the sun, Jake accepts the fact that for reasons he does not yet understand, God has sent Saul, Paul, whatever you want to call him, back to Earth. Not just back to Earth, but to him specifically. He doesn't know what this means for him, but he does know it is, as Peter called it, an honor, and he should treat it as one from now on.

11

"Open Studio"

"You know I love looking at art," Julia says, becoming exasperated with Sal's resistance.

"Sure," he says, "in museums. I'm fine with that. But not at a rival bookstore with a grumpy-ass owner."

Julia had recently seen an announcement in the *Fort Worth Roundup* (sister publication to the also-free weekly paper *The Dallas Free Press*) that there would be an art studio opening in the back section of The Globe Bookshop. Sal was being difficult, however.

"You said you liked his store," she argues, "and that it wasn't really a competitor because he has stuff we don't and vice versa. I think adding an art studio to it is brilliant."

"I think it's weird," he says, already knowing this is a battle he will lose.

"The ad said there would be free beer."

"Fine," he replies. "But I'm not wearing a tie. Not for that part of town."

The Globe Bookshop is packed when Sal and Julia arrive, and Sal grumbles about the lack of parking as they walk the half-block to the store, past a yoga studio, hair salon and an equally packed gay bar that he had not noticed the first time he was down here. A young black woman in a cheerleader outfit wobbles into the bar as they pass, unsteady on very high heels.

"Why the hell is she dressed like that?" he asks. Julia stares at him in disbelief, then bursts out laughing.

"Probably because 'she' is actually a 'he,' and not used to the torture that is high heels," she replies. "As for the cheerleader costume, I am guessing there's a drag show tonight."

"That was a dude?" "I thought it was just a really unattractive woman. Nice legs though."

"That's more your type of place," she says with a grin, pointing to a country bar across the street. "In fact, I bet Ben will be there later tonight."

"A gay country bar? John Wayne is spinning in his grave."

As soon as they enter the store, Sal sees the wisdom of how much open space Paco has left in his arrangement of the bookcases. Though his own store is much larger, The Last Word would never hold this many people comfortably. Julia's gaze is immediately drawn to a series of three paintings depicting bright red lips against a plain white background. Sal leaves her there to find the bar.

He is making his way through the crowd, quite a few of whom he recognizes as customers of his, when Paco appears beside him.

"If only I had this many people in here all the time," he says, handing Sal a Rolling Rock. The green bottle is ice cold and dripping with condensation. "Though there are times when I'm content for it to just be me, Wendy, the books, and the art. She calls it the best clubhouse ever."

"I get both of those," Sal says after taking a swig. "We have to have customers, but my favorite time is at night when I'm alone in the shop. Really great turnout tonight, though."

"No surprise there," he replies. "Wendy's a genius and she knows more people than you and I ever will. She's sold art all over the country, and would have been even better known if she would have just left this damn town for New York years ago." He pauses and looks around at the art that has been hung on the walls or displayed on easels. "Glad she didn't, though. She's my best friend. I'd miss her."

Sal looks toward the back of the shop where an alcove has been transformed into a working studio. He can only see part of it from where they are.

"She may be your best friend, but aren't you giving up some prime selling space for that studio?"

"Nah," Paco replies, stroking his white beard. "This is more of a draw for the place than a few more books would be. Besides, it gives her a place to work away from her house, which is where her studio has been forever. Besides, watching her work inspires me to write more."

"You're a writer?" Sal asks, truly surprised.

"Isn't everybody? I'm not very good, but compared to Hemingway and Fitzgerald, who is?"

"I should introduce you to my employee Heather. You two would hit it off great."

A tall woman with wavy brown hair appears at Paco's side. The look of both satisfaction and relief on her face as she scans the crowd tells him immediately that this is the artist.

"Sal," Paco says, "this is the amazing Wendy. We've been friends for longer than you've been alive."

She extends her hand and shakes his firmly.

"Thanks for coming," she says. "Buy some art and drink some beer; we have plenty of both. The beer is actually from my husband's personal stock at the house – he's the bartender tonight – and there are some interesting varieties." She cuts her eyes toward the bar, which has been tucked in back in the Asian literature section.

"You're the gangster, right?" she continues. "I've been to your store a few times, though not as much lately as when I was younger and your uncle still ran it. Franklin was such a wonderful old scoundrel."

"Were you ever a Siren?" Sal asks without thinking. She smiles mischievously.

"No, but not for lack of him trying. Three or four of my sorority sisters were though."

Julia joins them, gushing for several minutes about various pieces she likes. After Wendy moves on to talk to some new arrivals, Julia pulls Sal back to the front of the shop.

"Look at this," she says, pointing to a painting on an easel near the front counter. "It looks just like the Chinese takeout box you described when you were griping that day about all the trash you found around the store, you know, the day the homeless guy was passed out in the alley. Like Camden and I don't find that and more every day."

The painting did look like the takeout box, exactly like it, in fact. There were actually two paintings side-by-side, one with the box and other things, including fortune cookies and their various fortunes slips, and one that was simply the box alone on off-white background. He likes that one better; it is roughly 12 inches by 12 inches, and would look great in the store. He motions Paco over.

"I'll take that one," he says.

"A fine choice. You can take it with you now or I can mark it 'sold' and you can come get it tomorrow. Frankly, the second option helps drive more sales."

"That's fine," Sal says, handing over several large bills. "And don't worry about the discount for a fellow bookseller."

"Never even crossed my mind," Paco says cheerfully as he slaps a 'sold' sign on the painting

Twenty minutes later, Sal and Julia are sitting in Luca's Pizza and Pasta next door to the Globe Bookshop, eating the best pizza Sal has tasted since leaving home. A gray-haired, barrel-chested man of about 60 stops at their table, pulls up a chair, and introduces himself.

"Luca Morelli," he says. "I own the place. I hope you two kids are enjoying the pizza." His age apparently allows him to get away with calling them kids.

"Everything is great," Julia replies.

"Best I've had since leaving Jersey," Sal adds. "This is Julia and I'm Sal."

"I know who you are, son," Luca says. "I had a pizzeria in Trenton before you were born."

Sal is stunned; he thinks hard, trying to recall a Luca's Pizza.

"I don't remember a Luca's. Was it called something else?"

"You don't remember because I was gone before you were old enough to chew. Your old man wanted more than I was willing to pay to keep the place 'safe from miscreants.' His words."

"Pop could turn a phrase," is all Sal can think to say to this. Julia shifts uneasily in her seat.

"I'm not bitter, though," Luca says with a broad smile. "Back home I was one of a thousand pizza joints, all excellent. Here I am a pearl among swine, the real deal. Did you know that half the pizzerias down here are run by Albanians? Albanians!"

Sal did not know this, and for a few minutes they commiserate on the decline of Italian-American civilization.

"I've got a good spot here," Luca says. "Near the hospital district, a high school, and the bookstore going in next door has helped. I'm not much of a reader myself, but I get traffic from there and Paco eats here every day."

"I would think you would also get good traffic from the two bars as well," Julia says. "Hungry drunks, after all."

"True. And it's actually three bars. The Day-Glo Lounge, that's the gay bar up the street; the Pink Saddle, that's the gay country bar across the street; and the 420 Club, that's the cinder block building across Pennsylvania. Easy to miss that one. It's a gay and straight bar that caters to the folks who live in the neighborhood."

"A gay and straight bar?" she asks, perplexed.

"Yeah," Luca says. "Both gay and straight people go there."

"Then wouldn't you just call it a bar?" she asks.

"Doll," he says in an exasperated tone, "did you not hear me say that gay people go in there too?"

"Luca," Sal says, "there has probably never been a bar in the history of bars that didn't have at least one gay patron. Probably a lot more than one."

Luca stares at him as if he's speaking Albanian.

"What Sal is saying," Julia says, since Luca seems dumbfounded, "is that gay people go to all bars, not just specifically gay ones."

Luca stands and shakes his head.

"Not in Trenton, they don't. Not in Trenton."

12

"The Way of Rome"

By the time Jake gets up, Saul has discovered infomercials, game shows, and a few video games that Jake would have thought much too violent for a person of his age and position. But they are tame when you consider that he had lived during a time when all wars were hand-to-hand combat and gladiatorial games were a form of entertainment. He has also found time to read all of his letters that made it into the New Testament, as well as Acts and the Gospel of Luke. He has just started back on the commentaries when Jake walks into the living room.

"As best I can tell," he says after happily devouring the banana Jake gave him along with an English muffin, "the letters you have from me are accurately translated. There are no gross mistranslations, in any case. I am concerned that the combination of two millennia's distance and the numerous letters you are missing could cause some significant cultural misunderstandings, however, and possibly some theological ones. You could very easily have the context completely wrong in some places."

"How would only having the letters we have cause theological issues?" Jake asks. "You just said that the ones you read appeared accurate as far as how they were translated."

"Think of it this way," he says, running a hand through his white beard. "Thirteen letters are all of my writing that survived, and you built a whole theological system around them. If 100 years from now I plucked out thirteen of your letters to pastors or churches, would those thirteen really give a full picture of who you were and what you believed? Maybe, and maybe not."

"A hundred years from now all of my correspondence will be gone," Jake replies, "since it's all electronic...emails and such...but I see your point." His head is starting to hurt thinking about all of the possibilities. He supposes that happens when it turns out that the bedrock you have stood on your entire life might actually be made of Jell-O.

"The good news," Saul continues, not realizing he has just made a pun, "is that Luke's Gospel is completely accurate, which probably means the others are as well. In the end, it doesn't matter as much what I had to say if you have Jesus' teachings."

"That's true," Jake admits.

"Do you have to go to the church today?" Saul asks. "If not, maybe we could go to the Catholic bookstore."

The day is filled with meetings Jake would be happy to avoid, and he's not preaching this weekend so he has no sermon to prepare. In the end it is the excitement in Saul's voice that clinches his decision. He calls the church and tells them he will be back in the morning, and then he and Saul head east to explore the wonders of the St. Iraneus Catholic Bookstore. It will turn out to be as much of a learning experience for Jake as it will for Saul.

.

Much like Damascus Road Christian Superstore, the St. Iraneus Catholic Bookstore is located in a strip mall. This strip mall, however, is not in an upscale neighborhood. The parking lot is filled with potholes and the lines of the parking spaces are faded to the point of invisibility. The building itself, a long one-story structure built in the early 1970s, badly needs a good power-washing.

The front door and glass display window of the store are plastered with various notices and posters, all advertising a concert or food drive or some other event for the local Catholic community. Once inside, Jake can't help but notice a difference in the atmosphere when compared to Damascus Road.

First of all, the store is less than a quarter of the size of its massive Protestant counterpart, though every nook and cranny is filled with goods. This gives the store the feel of an old resale shop rather than the sterile corporate vibe of the wide, orderly aisles of Damascus Road. There are only three employees visible, as opposed to the army of staff Damascus Road employs. Like Damascus Road, St. Iraneus has a wide selection of books, including Bibles, though the variety of Bibles is significantly smaller.

There are also a large number of items you would never find in an Evangelical bookstore: statues of saints (including, as Sal had mentioned to the nun, one of St. Joseph you are supposed to bury in your yard to ensure the quick sale of your house), prayer cards with images of the Virgin Mary, coins with the likenesses of current and former Popes engraved on them, and vials of holy water.

The single biggest difference between the two stores, however, is a small, hand-lettered sign that hangs above the cash register at the front of the store:

**We Are a Non-Profit Ministry
All Profits Donated Directly To
Catholic Charities of Texas**

This stuns Jake; he knows for a fact that Damascus Road is not non-profit, nor are any of the other large Christian bookstores in the area. He turns to one of the employees, a lady in her 60s wearing a long plaid dress.

"The store is non-profit?" he asks, indicating the sign.

"Yes, sir," she says brightly.

"So you're a volunteer?"

"No," she says, laughing and shaking her head. "It seems like it sometimes, but no. We all work for minimum wage, including the manager. That keeps the costs down and the profits, such as they are, up."

"How do you live on minimum wage?"

"Most of us are retired," she explains, "except for two young ladies that are still in high school. None of us have to count on this to keep a roof over our heads, or we wouldn't be here."

"I see," he says. "A very admirable ministry."

"How could we do it any other way?" she asks. "I wouldn't feel right profiting off the sale of things people need for their spiritual health. Fortunately I am in a position to donate all of my meager check back to the store."

At that point she has to help a customer who is looking for a scapular. Jake looks around for Saul and finds him standing by a shelf of figurines; they are statues of saints. He is holding one in his hand when Jake walks up to him.

"This doesn't look anything like me," he says, showing Jake the plaster figurine. He's right; it doesn't look anything like him.

"Why are you surprised?" Jake asks. "No one knows what you looked like. It's not like we have photographs of people from the first century."

"Hmmm," he says, then picks up a different statue. This one is labeled "St. Peter." Saul begins to laugh.

"What?" Jake asks.

"Peter's nose was a lot bigger than this, and his eyes were closer together," he says once he regains his composure. Then in a whisper he adds: "He was not a pretty man."

Jake has no response for this; though it indeed looks nothing like the vision who visited him, he is certainly not joining in on the mocking of an apostle. Instead he walks over to a shelf of books marked "Apologetics." There had been a huge section on Apologetics and Evangelism at Damascus Road Bookstore, but he had seen no need to point it out to Saul. The greatest defender of the faith in church history needed no instruction on telling people about Jesus from a bunch of 21st century writers.

The books in this section all approach the presentation of the Gospel from the Catholic viewpoint, just as the ones at Damascus Road (and the store inside Briarwood) come at it from an Evangelical worldview. And just as Evangelicals have books explaining in great detail why Catholicism was wrong in many of its practices, here they have several explaining the ways in which Protestants have veered from the One True Path. One in particular catches his eye, because the cover shows what appears to be a preacher at a pulpit in the foreground with St. Peter's Basilica in Rome in the background. The title is *Why Southern Baptists Exist: An Explanation in Six Words.* Jake has just started reading the publisher's blurb on the inside flap when someone behind him speaks.

"It's a very good book," the man says, "and quite well reasoned."

Jake turns, expecting to find an employee, though he had only seen females up to that point. Instead he finds himself looking up into the brilliant blue eyes of a gentleman who stands at least six foot six. He is dressed in black pants, a black button-up shirt, and black shoes. The only piece of clothing that is not black is his white clerical collar. Yep, he's a priest.

His eyes widen a bit when Jake turns to face him, and he knows immediately what that means: he recognizes him. It doesn't happen often, but it does happen. How in the world is he going to explain this? *You see, Father, I know I'm a Baptist preacher, but the Apostle Paul has returned to earth and wanted to see what one of your bookstores was like. Oh, and the statues don't look anything like the real guys.* Actually, he might not find Saul's presence as surprising as Jake does, being predisposed to belief in the saints and all.

To Jake's surprise he doesn't call him out as an infidel in their midst, nor give any further indication that he recognizes him. He simply continues talking about the book he still holds in his hands.

"I would be happy to buy it for you," he says. "I have no doubt you would find it more interesting than most of the store's regular customers."

His eyes glint when he says this; now he's mocking Jake. Or is he? He really can't tell for sure.

"So what are these six magic words the title refers to?" Jake asks, ready to counter them with his many years of experience as a preacher, evangelist, and missionary. The answer catches him completely off guard.

"It's actually three sets of two words each," the priest answers. "And I only tell you that because I know it will make it impossible for you *not* to read the whole thing. The six words are: German Princes, English Divorce, and American Slavery." He starts to turn away at that point, and in spite of himself Jake stops him.

"Wait one minute, Father," he says, the word "Father" sounding strange in his ears. "You can't just drop something like that on me without elaborating a little. I will agree to let you buy the book if you give a thumbnail summary. I have so little time to read lately I might be retired before I make good on the promise, but I will. Eventually."

The priest smiles, showing perfect, gleaming white teeth. Between his eyes and that smile, Jake imagines that a great number of his single female parishioners curse the Vatican's continued ban on priests marrying.

"I suppose I could give you the CliffsNotes version," he replies. "Would you like to walk across the parking lot to the Starbucks?"

A joke immediately leaps into Jake's mind: A priest, a preacher, and an apostle walk into a coffee house. He nods, gives him the book so he can pay for it, and retrieves Saul from the section selling medallions. He is still complaining that Saints Christopher, Jude, and Anthony are all better represented on the shelves than he is as Jake ushers him out the door.

13

"Six Magic Words"

Since Father Rory – they learned his name on the walk across the parking lot – had paid for the book, it is only right that Jake pay for the coffee. He introduces Saul as his uncle again, and as he does not protest Jake assumes he is in no rush to reveal himself even to the Church of Rome.

They sit in three of the ubiquitous overstuffed chairs, a small round table between them, with the sounds of smooth jazz wafting from the store's sound system. Father Rory had recently been transferred to a parish in Fort Worth from a much smaller church in the Texas Hill Country, and it was there several years before that he had first seen Jake preaching a revival at a high school stadium. "I went so I could scout the opposition, so to speak," the priest explains.

"So tell me about the six words, Father," Jake says once the small talk is over. "You said they were German Princes, English Divorce, and American Slavery. Doesn't sound very theological to me."

"That's the whole point," Father Rory replies, blowing on his pumpkin spice latte to cool it. "It's not theological at all, but rather historical, political, and economic."

"Money makes the monkey dance," Saul says. Rory and Jake both look at him. "Sorry, heard that on a game show I saw this morning."

Father Rory chuckles, and then continues. "You don't seem like one of those Baptists who believe that your denomination was founded by John the Baptist," he says.

"No," Jake says. "Those folks are thankfully an extremely small, fringe element."

"What about *The Trail of Blood* view?" he asks.

Jake shakes his head no, and then turns to Saul. "*The Trail of Blood*," he explains, "was a book written by a Baptist minister in the 1930s attempting to show a direct succession of Baptist churches from the time of Jesus to the present day. It winds its way through a bunch of dubious sects in order to make the case that Baptists evolved completely outside of the Catholic Church. It's complete nonsense."

"Therefore," the priest says, "you must hold the view, historically speaking, that the Baptist church broke from the Catholic Church."

"In broad terms, yes," Jake responds. "There are several steps in between that you have left out, like the Reformation and the Church of England. Most agree that the Baptist church was founded by John Smyth in 1606 as a breakaway from the Church of England."

Father Rory nods and takes a drink of his latte, which is now cool enough to not scald his tongue. He is pleased with this answer.

"I'm happy to see you hold the conventional view of your history," he says, flashing that megawatt smile. "It will make explaining the book much easier."

"I don't see how my view of history is going to make any difference," Jake replies. "I don't hold to Evangelical theology because of history, but because it's biblically sound."

Saul chuckles softly at this. Jake hears him, but doesn't think Father Rory does.

"Indulge me for just a few minutes and put what may or may not be biblically sound to one side," the priest says.

"I'll do my best," Jake says.

"Good, and in return I will try to keep this a brief as possible. In a nutshell, the premise of *Why Southern Baptists Exist: An Explanation in Six Words* follows a logical progression, and one I think you will find hard to dispute. It starts with, as I mentioned, German Princes. Many times over the centuries someone, in this case Martin Luther, saw problems with the church and attempted to break with Rome. Most ended up being burned as heretics."

"Yeah," Jake says. "Tolerant bunch of guys there in the Vatican." Rory ignores this and continues.

"Luther faced a similar fate," he says, "but he was saved by the intervention of Frederick III, Elector of Saxony, who hid him away in his castle while Luther worked on the German translation of the New Testament."

"Nothing new here, Father," Jake says.

"Not new perhaps, but a key fact has often been overlooked. Frederick did not save Luther from execution out of religious piety. He saw Luther's rebellion against Rome as a way for himself, and all of the other leaders of the many German principalities, to escape from the Pope's control. Remember that during this time the Pope was the ultimate authority in all things. Through the monasteries he controlled the best lands in Europe, taxed the people, and could excommunicate even kings. Frederick and his allies wanted those lands, taxes, and political power, so they supported Luther and created a German-centric version of Christianity."

"So you're saying that without the princes the Reformation fails," Jake says.

"Fails, or at least is postponed long enough for reforms to the Church that were truly needed to be enacted."

"That's a pretty simplistic explanation, but I suppose the book has more detail. What about the divorce thing, though I think I know where that's headed."

"Of course you do," Father Rory says. "King Henry VIII of England and Anne Boleyn. Most today think that England was on board with Luther at the time of the Reformation, but nothing could be further from the truth. With the help of Sir Thomas More, a young Henry wrote a scathing attack on Luther which earned him the title of

Defender of the Faith from the Pope. England should be Catholic today, just like France and Spain, but unfortunately Catherine of Aragon could not produce a male heir, and the Pope wouldn't grant Henry an annulment. Henry may have been against Luther's teachings, but he was against his dynasty dying with him even more."

"So he divorces Catherine, marries Anne, and sets himself up as the head of the Church of England," Jake says.

"Correct," Rory replies. "A church whose liturgy is, even today, more like the traditional Catholic service than you find in Catholic churches."

"What you're saying is that if Henry gets his divorce, England stays Catholic and Smyth never established the first Baptist church. A bit of a stretch, but possible."

"The final two words," the priest says, "and the ones that specifically deal with the Southern Baptist Convention, should be plain to you."

Jake has to admit that they are. In 1845, American Baptists in the southern states split with their northern counterparts over what is today an embarrassing issue. Baptists in these slave-holding states not only defended the institution of slavery (on the basis of a curse Noah placed on his son, Ham) but also the right for overseas missionaries to take their slaves to the mission field with them as they would any other property.

Jake explains all of this to Saul, who seems unsurprised. Of course, he was the one who admonished slaves to obey their masters in one of his letters.

"So you see," Father Rory says, "your beloved denomination only exists because of some very specific and very random events that have nothing to do with the teachings of Christ."

He is right, but Jake is irritated by his smug tone. He has a historical event of his own that he can point to, and does.

"I have two more words that the author of your book conveniently forgot," he says.

The priest raises one eyebrow, then motions with his free hand inviting Jake to continue.

"Constantine's conversion," Jake says. "If the Emperor had not declared Christianity to be the official religion of the Roman Empire, the institution we know today as the Catholic Church would never have existed. It was the Roman elite that created the Vatican hierarchy and all that goes with it."

"The Church existed from the moment Jesus appointed St. Peter as its head," he retorts.

Saul begins laughing, and not softly. His laughter grows loud enough that other customers look over at them.

"What's so funny?" Jake asks.

"You're both idiots," Saul replies. "The Way was never meant to be a worldly institution in constant conflict within itself; you made this happen with your stupid squabbles over the centuries. And I seem to recall a letter from the church's earliest days that addressed this very issue." He seemed to be thinking hard about the words, then began to speak again. "Brethren, some from Chloe's household have told me that there are disputes among you. One of you says, 'I follow Paul'; another, 'I follow Apollos'; another, 'I follow Peter'; and yet another, 'I follow Christ.' Is Christ divided? Was Paul crucified for you?" When he finishes he stares at them, inviting them to challenge him. Neither does.

The priest looks at his watch and stands up quickly. "I'm going to be late for an appointment," he says. "I've enjoyed talking to you both, and would love to discuss this further sometime." He shakes hands with each of them and then leaves the Starbucks.

"You certainly shot us down with that quote from Corinthians," Jake says.

"That's not important now," Saul says. "We have much more important things to attend to than the priest."

"What, you're not here for the Catholics too, just us Evangelicals?"

"Peter is better at dealing with the Catholics than I am," Saul says. "They respond much better to him, for obvious reasons. But right now I'm hungry."

"You're always hungry," Jake says. "What do you want this time?"

"Catfish," he replies without hesitating. "I want to try catfish, and hushpuppies."

"Fine," Jake says, trying to think of the nearest seafood place. "And I suppose you don't want shrimp or any shellfish, right?"

"Shellfish is ok," he says.

"Picking and choosing on the dietary laws again, are we?" Jake asks with a smirk. "Very convenient."

"I highly doubt a man as clearly spiritual as yourself would be tripped up by something as insignificant as a few shrimp or some fried oysters."

"You never know," Jake retorts. "I might have a very weak faith. The smallest dab of tartar sauce could send me spiraling into a pit of decadence and debauchery."

"That's a risk I am willing to take," Saul says with a broad smile. "After all, once I'm gone I may never get to sample these fine foods again. It would be inhospitable of you to deny me the pleasure."

"I suppose it would," Jake says, deciding on Martin's Fish House on Lancaster. "And never let it be said that Jake Donovan is an inhospitable host. My dear departed mother would be ashamed."

"Yes," Saul agrees. "That would be very bad indeed."

14

"A Day of Librarians"

Sal steps through the front door of The Globe Bookshop the next morning, straight into a heated exchange between Paco and a female customer.

"You need more female authors who can write female characters," the woman says forcefully. "The last book I got here took almost 50 pages before there was a substantive conversation involving a woman."

"Don't talk to me," Paco says, his tone even. "Talk to the female authors. They all write Romances because that's where the money is."

"That is the most sexist —"

"Calm down," he says, cutting her off. "It is not my fault that God, in his wisdom, made women inferior to men. You should just be glad we were magnanimous enough to finally elevate you above the status of property."

Her eyes bulge; she sputters a few incomprehensible words and storms out the door. Paco takes a sip of his coffee, finally noticing Sal. He nods his head slightly.

"What the hell?" Sal asks.

"That was nothing," he says. "We have the same argument every week. Usually she throws a Hemingway novel at me."

"Because she thinks he was a misogynist?" Sal ventures.

"That's part of it, sure. But also because she's a vegan."

"I don't get it."

"The whole bullfighting obsession he has," Paco explains. "She objects to it as a vegan."

"But they don't ever eat the bulls," Sal says.

"I know. Maybe it's a PETA thing too. Who knows? The important thing is that she always buys her books – lots of them – before we fight. Wish I had a hundred customers like her, but there aren't that many librarians in this town. So what brings you back down here? Slumming?"

"Man, your customer service skills need work," Sal says. "I tried calling so I wouldn't have to drive down here, but apparently you don't answer your phone. I wanted to ask you about your experience hosting local author events, signings and readings and such. I saw that you do a lot of them."

"I do indeed. Don't you?"

"Not really," Sal admits. "We do story time because the kids love me, and we get some of the few major authors that actually still do book tours, but nothing with the local writers."

Paco nods, pulls out a pack of Camels, and points at the door. Sal joins him out front. Jennings Avenue is deserted; it is too early for the lunch crowd at Luca's, and much too early for any of the bar patrons. Paco motions down the street with his left arm, ash falling from the cigarette as he does so.

"This is why I have to host the local authors and you don't," he says. "You get foot traffic all day; people have to make an effort to get to me."

"So you don't like doing it?" Sal asks.

"Oh, I like it fine," he replies. "There are some extremely talented local authors who simply can't break into traditional publishing because they aren't writing the right thing: wizard fantasies, unreliable-narrator thrillers, vampire sex books, etc. So they just indie publish."

"You say some," Sal observes. "So not all?"

"Good Lord no," Paco laughs. "Some is total crap. I always look over the books first before agreeing to a signing. A lot of times the more professional the thing looks on the outside, the better the writing is likely to be on the inside; in this case you can judge a book by its cover. Hosting the event is a win-win; they get to promote their book in a real store and I get a crowd of people who buy other books while they're here. And they usually bring booze."

"So because they're local it guarantees a good turnout?" Sal asks, clearly pondering the advantages of this.

"I wish," Paco says, flicking a cigarette butt into the street. "I promote all the events, but they have to get their friends and family here. Had one poor guy, whose book had been out for a while, who had his signing on a night we had a massive thunderstorm. No one came."

"No one?"

"Not a single person walked through the door for two hours. Not even to get in from the rain."

"Ouch."

"Yeah. It can be hit-or-miss. Just like life."

Back at The Last Word, Sal is looking through a massive stack of indie-published books the store has received over the past few months. He starts by culling out the ones from outside Texas they have received by mail – have to keep it local – but this only reduces the pile by a few. He's just started sorting them into piles by genre when a statuesque blond bursts through the door and heads straight for him. This cannot be good.

"Sal Terranova," she says. It is not a question.

"That's me," he replies. "What can I do for you?"

If looks could kill, Sal would be dead already. She doesn't reply immediately, and he wracks his brain trying to recall the woman and what he may have done to so enrage her. Glancing down, he notices she has a tattoo on her left inner forearm: it is in the classic typewriter font and is a single word: bibliophile. Now he knows he's never met her; he would remember that tattoo.

"I would like to know," she says, her voice suddenly calm and soft, which makes her far scarier, "where you get off telling everyone that Fort Worth needs to be known as a book town and you're going to make that happen?"

"I –"

"The sheer arrogance of such a statement simply defies description."

"I –"

"Who made you the guardian of all things bookish in this town?"

"If you would just let me speak," he says as she finally draws in a breath.

"Fine," she says, crossing her arms and taking a defiant stance. "Speak."

"First off," he says, "you clearly know who I am. Who are you, if I may ask?" The question surprises her; she obviously expected a belligerent response out of the gate.

"Oh," she says, reflexively dropping her arms and then extending her hand. "I'm C.K. Webster."

Sal shakes her hand; she has a firm grip and, he also notes, piercing eyes that have transformed from hazel to greenish as her demeanor changed.

"It's a pleasure to meet you," he says sweetly. "And while I disagree totally with your initial characterization of my book-related efforts, I am happy to discuss it with you. What exactly is your interest in the matter?" He has, as he hoped, surprised her again, this time with the fact that he used the word "characterization." She has not let go of his hand. She realizes this and quickly withdraws hers.

"I'm the Director of Acquisitions for the Fort Worth Public Library System," she replies.

"Ah," Sal says. "I knew I recognized the name, but I've never seen your face. They really should put pictures on the website."

This time he has taken the flattery one step too far. Her eyes narrow suspiciously, and he fears she may think he is simply dismissing her. He moves on quickly.

"I am certainly not the guardian of all things bookish in this town," he assures her. "I'm barely the guardian of things in my own store. But yes, I do hope to help make Fort Worth a book town."

C.K. smiles, much like a cobra would smile at a mouse.

"There's the arrogance again," she says, though at least now her tone is not so angry. "Why do you think we are not already a book town? We have one of the finest public library systems in the state, maybe even the country."

Now Sal understands. He has, however unintentionally, offended this woman as a *librarian*, someone who has certainly spent much more of her life in the promotion of books and defense of intellectual freedom than he has.

"You're absolutely right about the quality of our libraries," he says. "I spend a fair amount of time there myself. However, I would argue that no matter how good a public library is, it can't make a place a book town."

"Why not?" she asks, her tone now intrigued rather than hostile.

"Because a public library is, by its very nature, a place for the residents of its community. A book town is, as much as anything else, a destination for people outside of its community. Think of it this way: except for the Library of Congress and the British Library, how many people, even bibliophiles – he nods at her arm – go to a public library in a city they are visiting on vacation? Not many. But book lovers flock to book stores wherever they go, especially if they happen to be somewhere known to be a book town."

"Like Hay-on-Wye or Wigtown in the UK," she says.

"Exactly."

She ponders this for a moment, trying to find a flaw in his argument, with no success. "I suppose when you put it that way," she says.

"Now I have a question for you," Sal says. "Why have I never seen you in my shop before today?"

She smiles, and it's a great smile this time.

"I shop local," she says. "And though I work in Fort Worth, I live in Cleburne, where we have a fine indie bookstore."

"Fair enough," he says. "But you're here now. How about I give you the nickel tour?"

"Why not," she agrees. "I have to admit that I've wanted to check out that new place on Jennings. My local store doesn't have much in translation."

"The Globe is a great store," Sal says as he steps from behind the counter. "But the owner is not nearly as pleasant as me."

15

"Give Me that Old-Time Religion"

Camden is amazed the next morning to find Sal not only already in the store but reorganizing the religion section. It is a good thing the store doesn't open for more than an hour, because it will take him at least that long just to get all of the books back on the shelves. She walks over to inspect what he is doing, and finds that he has also removed a large number of books from surrounding sections as well. He has not touched fiction, of course, not wanting to incur the wrath of Heather.

"What are you doing?" she asks?

"Making space for more Bibles," he says as he drops several books on numerology into a bin labeled "Clearance."

"Why are you doing that?" she asks, "And why are those books going on clearance?"

"They should just be donated to Goodwill for the tax write-off," he says. "They've been here since we took over the store. "I am doing it because we are expanding the religion section. There is a vast, untapped market that is driving right past our store every day to the monstrosity that is Damascus Road Christian Superstore."

"What in the world are you on about now?" she asks. "If this is another church scheme I will go and get the nun right now."

"It's not a scheme at all," he says, tossing more books into the clearance pile. "It's business, plain and simple."

"Explain then."

He stands up and considers his progress thus far; still a lot more to do, and almost no way to finish before the store opens.

"Be a peach and make me a cup of coffee," he says. "I'll be glad to give you all the details."

She does not want to get him coffee, but she does want the details, so she agrees, grumbling the whole way. When she returns with the cup, he has cleared even more shelves.

"Shouldn't you be putting things back on the shelf at this point?" she asks. "We'll be open soon."

"Can't be helped," he says as he sets a volume on tantric sex to one side.

"Is that going in the clearance pile as well?"

"Nope," he says with a sly grin. "That one's going to Julia's with me tonight."

"Ick. I do not want to hear that." She takes a seat on the floor next to him, trying not to knock over the growing towers of books. "Now tell me what this is all about."

"I was talking to Heather the other day," he says after taking a sip of the coffee and nodding approvingly. "She told me about her trip down to Damascus Road with Saul – no pun intended – and Jake. She went on and on about how much stuff they had, how many people were in there, how we were missing out on sales. So I decided to go check it out myself."

"You went to a Christian bookstore?"

"I did indeed," he says. "But I made Jake go with me. I was afraid of what might happen if I went in alone; it's a known fact that some of those Evangelical types don't like Catholics." She rolls her eyes. "What?" he asks. "It's true."

"How would they know you're a Catholic, Sal?"

"Oh they would know, trust me. They can smell a potential convert a mile away, which is why I wanted one of their own with me. Anyway, Heather wasn't kidding; the place is amazing, from a strictly crass, commercial point of view at least."

"I still don't see what that has to do with us," Camden says.

"It has everything to do with us," he replies, standing up and stretching the muscles in his back. "We are supposed to be the go-to place for books for all of the people who live downtown, yet when they want Bibles or other Christian reading matter they drive right past our door on their way to Damascus Road. I don't even want to think about how many sales we're losing, and those Bibles are not cheap. And guess what else I learned."

"What?" she asks.

"There is no sales tax on Bibles," he says. "We can make a profit and the government gets zilch. I do love the separation of church and state."

Camden sighs and looks around at the mess he has made. He is probably right that they are missing sales, but she also isn't sure that the kind of people who shop at Damascus Road would buy a Bible from them. She decides to hold off saying this for now, since he seems so pleased with his new project. And at least this one isn't illegal.

Later, when business slows down a bit, Camden and Julia walk over to check on Sal, who is now fighting a hell of his own creation. He has removed the books he wants to get rid of, and has a good idea of what he wants the new section to look like. What he lacks are the books to fill it; he has not ordered any of the numerous types of Bibles they stock at Damascus Road because he frankly has no clue where to start. He is saved, so to speak, by the arrival of Jake and Saul.

"I knew you had no idea what to order," Heather says as she walks over to Sal, "so I called Jake to see if he can help you out. I'm not sure that your plan will work, but if we're going to do it, we need to do it right."

Jake walks over to them, but Saul heads straight for the rare book room. He apparently prefers Jacob's company to taking part in this blatant commercialization of the Word of God. Jake hands Sal a sheet of paper.

"Here's a list of what you should start with," he says, "at least as far as Bibles and commentaries. I also added some popular titles by Beth Moore – the women really love her stuff – as well as Max Lucado, Jim Cymbala, and Francis Chan. That should cover you for a while."

"No Joel Swindon?" Sal asks. "I've actually heard of him, and his books are everywhere, even at the supermarket."

"Heretic!" Saul screams from across the room. For an old man his hearing is excellent.

"Saul doesn't approve of Swindon," Jake says with a laugh.

"Do you really think anyone is going to come here for these books?" Julia asks. She has been skeptical since Sal told her his idea, which surprised him since she is at least nominally Baptist.

"I am sure of it," he says. "I did some research, and I found some very interesting things that I believe will work in our favor."

"Like what?" Camden asks, leery of Sal's "research."

"First of all, most know that the Bible is the best-selling book of all time," he says.

"Most?" Heather asks. "Doesn't everyone know that?"

"Sadly, no," he says, shaking his head. "There are some who would say *The Da Vinci Code,* one of the Harry Potter books, or even *The Forbidden Fruit.* Sadly, my research shows that although it's still the best-selling, it's also likely the least-read book in America today." Jake nods at this.

"What does that mean?" Heather asks.

"It means we're Bible-illiterate," he says. "To borrow the line from a less biblical question, 90% of people don't read the Bible, and the other 10% lie about it. Even here in the Bible Belt most only dust their copy off long enough to carry into Sunday services. Then they toss it into the back seat of their SUV until the next week."

"He's right about that too," Jake says.

"It's worse than that," Jacob informs them. He and Saul have left the safety of the rare book room and joined them. "My generation was at least familiar with most of the Bible stories, if not the theology. That's not true anymore, and if you think I'm exaggerating, consider the following responses to some simple Bible knowledge questions I heard the other day on one of those late-night talk shows. People said things like 'in the first book of the Bible, Adam and Eve were created from an apple tree,' and 'Moses went up on Mount Cyanide to get the Ten Commandments and died before he ever reached Canada,' and 'Lot's wife was a pillar of salt during the day, but a ball of fire at night.' My two favorites were 'Noah's wife was Joan of Ark,' and 'it was a miracle when Jesus rose from the dead and managed to get the tombstone off the entrance.' These are the people who will be running this country some day. Thank God I won't be alive to see it."

To everyone's surprise, Saul starts laughing, and laughs so hard for a time that they are worried he might crack a rib or something. He finally regains his composure and wipes the tears from his eyes.

"A pillar of salt during the day, but a ball of fire at night," he repeats. "I have to tell Peter that one."

"I still don't see why you care about any of this," Camden says to Sal. "Apart from the money aspect anyway."

"I care," Sal explains, "because the issue of Biblical illiteracy goes hand in hand with our growing illiteracy overall. Whatever your religious affiliation, the fact is many of our laws are based on the Bible, and much of our great art and literature was inspired by the Bible. Not knowing anything at all about the Bible is as unacceptable as knowing nothing about the Constitution, Shakespeare, or Michelangelo."

"Well said, son" Jacob says with an approving nod.

Heather turns to Jake, who is staring at Sal as if he cannot believe he had such a lucid and well-reasoned response.

"Is there any fiction on that list?" she asks.

"He told me none of the Christian fiction was any good," Saul says, remembering their conversation at Damascus Road.

"Not all of it is bad," Jake says. "Obviously the Narnia books are classics."

"We already have those," she says.

"Frank Peretti and Ted Dekker both have some good novels," he continues. "My favorite 'Christian' novels are the *Flabbergasted* trilogy by Ray Blackston."

"What are they about?"

"The trials and tribulations of a group of twenty-something Presbyterian singles in South Carolina who use Sunday School singles' classes to get dates."

"Actually sounds interesting," she replies, and then with a wink she adds "I'll have to come by your place soon and borrow them."

16

"Black"

Jake walks into the waiting room of Dr. Jenret's office, and is surprised to see someone he recognizes sitting there reading a months-old copy of *Sports Illustrated*. The man lives in Jake's neighborhood and works at the resale shop not far from his loft. He can't remember his name, though, and he must have been staring at him without realizing it.

"Eli," the man says, placing the magazine back on the small end table. "My name's Eli."

"Sorry," Jake says. "I'm bad with names." He actually isn't bad with names, but this guy is utterly forgettable.

"I'm used to it," he says without a hint of self-pity. He seems to want to say more, but hesitates.

"Yeah," Jake says, fairly sure what he's thinking. "It's weird running into someone you know at your shrink's office. But here we are. So what's your malfunction?"

"I get letters from a girl who lived more than 100 years ago," he says with a shrug.

"Nice," Jake replies. "I miss killing people and currently have the Apostle Paul as a houseguest."

Eli stares at him, apparently not sure if he is serious. When he decides he is, his response is short and to the point.

"You win," he says, and picks up the magazine again.

At that moment the door to Dr. Jenret's office opens. She steps out, sees the two of them, and looks as if she might cry.

"I am so sorry about this," she says, turning to Jake. "My schedule is completely off and I've had people double booked all day and..."

He holds up his hand and she stops talking, which has never happened before.

"It's fine," he says. "I can come back later, or I can wait until you finish with this gentleman." He nods at Eli. "I have no other pressing engagements at the moment."

She smiles and nods. That could mean anything, but Jake chooses to take a seat and wait; he really wants to talk to her about Saul. Eli stands, gives Jake a half nod, and walks into the office after her. A minute later she reappears holding a sheet of paper.

"I've been meaning to have you fill this out," she says, handing it to him, "but I keep forgetting about it. It's a different kind of assessment tool. Why don't you do it while you wait?"

He glances at the paper, then back at her. He hates these things, and she knows he hates them. Before he can protest she vanishes back into her office. He pulls out a pen, but has no intention of submitting quietly.

The heading reads "Colors," and there are only seven questions. This is a surprise; shrinks like lots of questions so they can have lots of data to misinterpret. He bends over the small coffee table, reads the first question, and begins to exact his revenge for having to wait behind Eli the forgettable clerk.

1. What is your favorite color? Why?

Black, because it matches my heart. Actually it matches everything, and with my fashion sense that's a plus. Musically speaking, it's just better; ask yourself: 'Back in Black' or 'Blue Eyes Crying in the Rain?', 'Paint It Black' or '99 Red Balloons'? Pearl Jam's 'Black', Amy Winehouse's 'Back to Black', and Metallica's Black album. And of course, Johnny Cash was the Man in Black.

2. Do you wear this color? How often and when?

Yes. Pretty much daily and everywhere. Typically the shirts and cowboy boots are black…and blue jeans, which does not mean I'm partial to blue. I'm partial to jeans…it's a Texas thing.

3. What does the color suggest to you?

Possibilities. Why is it that only a white canvas can be considered blank?

4. What does it not suggest to you?

Evil, melancholy, darkness, or any of the other reasons teenagers and horror writers like it. Darth Vader was a badass in black, while Luke Skywalker was a wimp in white.

5. How long has it been your favorite color?

It was always among my favorites, but it rocketed to the top when I realized it made me look less fat.

6. When does it not work for you?

In the shower.

7. How does the color relate to you, or you to it? Are you this color or is this color you?

Colors don't typically relate to me, and I don't work, play, or relate well with anyone, including colors. I am not this color (though I wanted to be Kareem Abdul-Jabbar when I was a kid playing basketball, if that means anything) and this color would likely not want to be me. We co-exist peacefully mainly because we're stuck together, like

Lennon and McCartney, Keith and Mick, Morrissey and Marr ... only with less drama.

Jake looks back over his answers, quite sure he has done little to further his "progress," but pleased with himself nonetheless. Maybe it's true that deep down all men are nothing more than 12-year-old boys.

"So, how have things been since our last meeting?" she asks once Eli is gone and Jake is seated comfortably on her couch. She is wearing an ankle-length skirt today, which makes Jake sad, though he doesn't say this.

Well let's see, he thinks. *I have seen visions and taken the Apostle Paul in as a roommate.* On the plus side he is dating a nice girl who may or may not be slightly insane.

"Not much," he says. It is entirely possible that his lack of progress in counseling stems from his inability to tell her what's really going on with him. But then she gives him something he can work with.

"At our last meeting," she says, looking at her notes, "you said that you thought you were starting to miss killing people, and then you had to leave. Let's explore that a little more."

"Sure," he replies. "Explore away."

"Why do you think you feel that way?"

"I was good at it. It's nice to be good at what you do."

"Yes it is," she says, nodding and writing in her notebook at the same time. "What else?"

He decides to give her the truth, which he usually tries to avoid when possible because it just makes her ask more questions.

"Have you ever had sex?" he asks, turning the tables on her.

"Well, yes, of course," she says, blushing a little.

"So you know that feeling right before and during climax?"

"Yes." She shifts in her chair a little.

"Ever had really great cheese enchiladas?"

"Uh, yes. Where are you going with this?"

"Just bear with me for a minute. Ever been on the beach in the fall when the sun is just coming up?"

"Actually, yes."

Jake looks at her coffee mug and notices that it has the Dallas Cowboys logo on it.

"Do you remember the Super Bowls the Cowboys won in the early 1990's?"

"Absolutely," she says. She smiles when she says it, and he knows she is remembering a moment from one of the games, maybe an Emmitt Smith touchdown run or a Charles Haley sack.

"Okay," he says. "Take all of those moments, add in the greatest thing you ever accomplished personally or professionally, and you don't even come close to the feeling you get in the milliseconds right before, during and immediately after you pull that trigger. There's a period there when the adrenaline from the anticipation of it disappears, and before the twinge of guilt afterward inevitably comes, that you get a rush that no drug or sexual experience or anything else can top."

She seems at a loss for words, which he has never seen before. He takes advantage of her silence and continues.

"For the greater part of my life I have been on a search for God. During those moments I just described, I *was* God. Because in the end, the closest we can come to the power of God is the power over life and death. And our ability to create life, since it's limited to the long process of conception and birth and has to involve two people, is not the same thing."

"And you miss that feeling, the feeling you had when you were in combat?" she asks.

"Yes, but combat was different. Combat is a blur of images and emotions and is another rush that no drug comes close to. But the feeling I'm talking about, the God-feeling, only came when I was on a mission to take out one person. It was more intimate, more of a one-on-one experience, done more slowly and more methodically."

She nods and writes quite a bit more. Jake wonders if doctor-patient confidentiality will prevent her from calling the FBI as soon as he leaves.

17

"The Pope Incident"

After his session with Dr. Jenret, Jake doesn't feel like going straight home. Instead he heads east on I-30, exiting at downtown Dallas. He passes through the triple underpass of Kennedy assassination fame and pulls up at an old warehouse near Dealey Plaza that has been renovated and now boasts high-dollar lofts and some offices. On the sixth floor are the offices of the *Dallas Free Press*, a weekly newspaper/tabloid that carries both insightful political commentary and ads for strip clubs and methadone clinics. His Uncle Zeke has been a writer there for the past 15 years, and since he works bizarre hours, Jake knows he will be there without calling first.

Zeke's desk is against a window that looks directly across at the sixth floor of the old Texas School Book Depository Building, from where, if you believed the official version, Oswald shot Kennedy. Jake isn't sure about the official version and had always been fascinated by the whole event, in no small part because at the very moment the President was pronounced dead in the ER at

Parkland Hospital, he was being born on a different floor in the same hospital.

Martin "Zeke" Donovan was something of an enigma in the Donovan family ("black sheep" barely scratched the surface), and his work area is a perfect example. Coffee mugs are everywhere, most still half-full, overflowing ashtrays (one under a No Smoking sign), pictures of him with Darrell Royal, Richard Nixon, Bill Clinton, Emmitt Smith, and amazingly, Fidel Castro, and two framed Pulitzer Prize awards. The first was a result of his first-hand account of the battle of Khe San in 1968, which he wrote while a Marine infantryman. The second came from an investigation into corruption in the City of Dallas, which was still his favorite subject. There was also a framed, signed photograph of Ronald Reagan with hundreds of pinholes in it.

With his resume, he could have gone to a paper in LA or New York or DC, but he said that being so close to Dealey Plaza, "where all history changed," inspired him. He had spent years at the old *Dallas Times-Herald*, where he won his second Pulitzer, but left when the paper merged with the *Dallas Morning News*. It helped that this paper was so far outside the mainstream that he could be as inflammatory as he wanted with little editorial censoring. He had his own website, and the national media still picked up some of his articles.

Jake leans across the desk to look at a photograph of Zeke and his dad taken on a fishing trip years ago, and as he does he feels a sharp pain in the back of his left arm. He reaches back and feels a small dart embedded in the skin, which he pulls out and throws on the desk.

"Sorry about that, Jake," Zeke says as he walks up to the desk. "I was aiming at the picture of Reagan."

They shake hands and hug in that arms' length way that men do, and as Zeke sits down behind the desk, Jake can tell that his uncle has changed since he'd seen him last. There is more salt than pepper in his hair and the slight roll around his midsection is evidence of his reduced gym time. The years show more in his face now, too, especially the lines around his eyes and the corners of his mouth. He has been too many places and seen too many things to age gracefully, but his hair is close-cropped and his face clean-shaven, which is an improvement. He wears faded jeans with sandals and a hideous Hawaiian shirt. He must own a hundred Hawaiian shirts.

"So what brings you downtown?" Zeke asks. He lights a Winston and takes a drink from one of the coffee mugs. "Already save all the souls in the suburbs?"

"Funny. Actually I just left the therapist's and wasn't ready to go home yet," he says, taking a cigarette from the pack on his desk.

"The one with the great legs? How's that going? You all cured?"

"Hardly. I told her that shooting people from long distances made me feel like God, which she took pretty well. I did not tell her that I now have the Apostle Paul as a roommate."

"Say again?" Zeke asked.

"I told her being a sniper was like being God."

"Not that. The other part."

"Oh. Yeah, Saul of Tarsus is my new best friend."

"You're going to have to explain that, nephew."

Jake gives him a thumbnail sketch of his experience with the old man claiming to be the second coming of history's greatest apostle. He expects a skeptical response, but is surprised.

"Let me interview him," Zeke says with a gleam in his eyes.

"Absolutely not," Jake says. "You've written some nutty things before, but putting that in print would top them all."

"When have I written a crazy story that involved you?" he asks, trying to look hurt.

"Do I have to remind you about the Pope incident?"

"I can't believe you're still upset about that," he says.

"Whatever. No Saul stories."

"All right, don't get so worked up. It's a shame, though."

Jake thinks back on "The Pope Incident" as he drives home. Looking back, it was a pretty funny story, but he didn't think so at the time. It had come during his period of trying to convert Catholics to the true Faith, not long after a spirited debate with a priest named Father Joey who was known more for his practical jokes than his piety. The priest came to his loft one day and asked if they could talk. Then he sat down on the couch and gave Jake what could only be considered a sinister smile.

"What did you do?" he had asked, not sure if he wanted to hear the answer.

"Nothing much, really," Joey replied, barely able to contain his laughter. "I think this press release will sum it all up for you."

He handed Jake a single page; it had been faxed from somewhere in Washington State. It read:

The One True Apostolic and Catholic Church announced today that the Conclave of Cardinals and Laity has chosen a successor to Pope Xavier IX. The new Holy Father is John Kennedy Donovan, and he has taken the name Pope Bruno I.

Jake hadn't read any further before dropping the paper on the coffee table. "No offense, Father, but what the hell is this?"

"You have been chosen as the successor to St. Peter."

"This is a joke, right?"

"Oh no, it's quite serious. And very official." He was laughing now.

"And ignoring for the moment that I've never heard of these people, how did *I* get elected? I'm not even a priest. I'm not even Catholic anymore."

"Neither are they, really, and being a priest is not a requirement. You've certainly exhibited that you are a committed evangelist. Of all my arguments for your election, I think that swayed them most. I also left out that you're now a Protestant."

"*Your* arguments? You're behind this insanity?" Jake had briefly considered leaping over the table and pummeling him; he was a lot smaller than Jake.

"I thought you'd be grateful. You've spent so many years trying to convert Catholics, and now you're in the unique position of being their leader, Your Holiness."

He laughed so hard as he said this that he fell off the couch. Jake pulled his Glock from its holster and laid it on the table; he stopped laughing.

"Before I shoot you, you're going to explain this whole thing to me. I guess the name is as good a place to start as any. Why Bruno I?"

"I told them that you wanted that name. Bruno is Italian for Bruce, and I knew you were a big Springsteen fan." In spite of the Glock, he started laughing hysterically again.

"You're telling me that I'm the Pope."

"Not *the* Pope exactly. More like an anti-pope. Obviously, the Vatican doesn't recognize you. In fact, they may declare you a heretic."

"Joey," he said, "you're gonna pay for this. Now tell me who these freaks are."

"They are a group of Catholics that want the pre-Vatican II ways reestablished, but with American-style democracy thrown in, which is why you don't have to be a priest. They're one of hundreds of small splinter groups all over the world. I chose them because they were in need of a Pope, as theirs had recently died in a freak golf cart accident."

This whole thing should have been nothing more than a very short-lived joke. Jake had even told a few people about it; unfortunately Zeke was one of them.

One particularly slow afternoon at the Blarney Stone a week later, Jake had been sitting at the bar with Ortiz, reading the sports section and sipping a Bailey's and coffee while Monica, the new bartender, made small talk with a banker drinking his lunch. She was the typical Eddie Donovan hire: young, beautiful, great legs, and small breasts. For whatever reason, his brother had always been turned off by well-endowed women, and never considered that his patrons wouldn't feel the same way.

Two young guys, probably in their mid-teens, opened the front door and peered inside. They walked in hesitantly, which confirmed that they were underage. One was clutching a newspaper.

"Need to see some ID," Jake said without looking up.

They both stopped and pulled out their drivers' licenses. Monica inspected them, found that they were indeed underage, and told them to get out. They both glanced over at Jake.

"But we're here to see him," one said.

Jake looked over, wondering what this could be about. They were young enough to be his kids, and at least one bore a slight resemblance to him. It was possible that his past had caught up with him, but unlikely. The other was medium height and stocky; he reminded Jake of the rugby players he had seen on a recent rerun of *Friends*. They were probably in a band looking for a gig.

"What can I do for you?" he asked, remaining seated. "As you can see, I'm fairly busy right now." Ortiz laughed and took the paper away from him.

They stepped toward him slowly, and the one who had spoken introduced himself as Joshua; the silent one's name was Byron. Joshua hesitated for a minute and then blurted out:

"Are you the Pope?"

Great, he thought. *As if I don't already have enough to deal with.*

"Do I look like the Pope?" he answered, hoping they'd just go away. The conversation turned Monica's attention away from the banker, and he also looked over, his ego deflated.

"Well," Joshua said, showing Jake the paper he was holding, "this picture looks an awful lot like you, and the article said you spent a lot of time in this place."

Jake took the paper from him. It was the most recent issue of *The Dallas Free Press*, and of course it was an article written by Zeke. On the cover was a picture of him from a few years back under the headline "The Lone Star Pope." He wondered if they would de-pope him after he killed Zeke a few hours from now.

"It's a joke, kid," he had said, tucking the paper under his coffee mug. He would check out the article when no one was around.

"I don't think so," Byron replied. "We checked it out on the Internet, and several sites said you were the new Pope. Even CNN. I never heard that the last one died, but I've been really busy lately."

These were the future leaders of America. He shuddered at the thought, stood up, and looked at them hard.

"Are you boys Catholic?"

"Yes, sir," they both answered. Joshua added "Your Excellency," perhaps unsure if "sir" was the proper way to address him.

"Then here's what I want you to do. Go back to your parish priest and tell him you came to see me. He'll tell you what to do next." Monica stifled a laugh and turned away, but the banker seemed transfixed by the whole scene.

The young men looked a little disappointed, but chose not to argue with their new Pontiff a second time. They turned to go, but when they got to the door, Byron stopped and looked back at him.

"Could you at least bless us, Pope Bruno?"

Why not? He thought. Jake walked over, put his hands on their bowed heads for a moment, made the sign of the cross over them, and told them to "Go with God." They left seeming quite satisfied with the experience.

As he sat back down, Monica leaned across the bar toward him.

"Wanna go in the back for a little while?" she asked with a mischievous grin.

"Why?" he asked.

"Hell, how many girls can say they nailed the Pope?"

The banker dropped his beer glass, astounded; it shattered on the floor.

"I'd love to my child," he answered, "but it would conflict with my vows."

"Would you settle for a Puerto Rican Bishop?" Ortiz asked. She smiled and nodded. He took her by the hand led her to Eddie's office.

All things being equal, it was a pretty good article. Zeke even took some quotes from an old sermon of Jake's and rearranged them to make it appear that he had accepted the position. The story stressed that the Vatican had no comment, other than to say that they already had a Pope, thank you very much. Zeke went on to write that this was more of a response than he had received from City Hall in years regarding their various screw-ups. He also quoted an anonymous priest who thought the election was a giant step forward for all of Christendom. Now, Jake thought as he read on, Joey needed to die as well.

The article and subsequent web and news coverage were sure to bring out every nut case within 500 miles, and Jake was certain that unless he acted fast, Eddie would set up a shrine on the stage to cash in on the free publicity. He could only imagine what his Evangelical friends would think.

He ultimately did the only thing he could do: he excommunicated the entire church, including himself. They responded by defrocking him. The last Jake heard, their new Pope was named Beatrice I. Very democratic.

18

"A Shakedown Goes Horribly Wrong"

Things are dead quiet at The Last Word on an overcast Tuesday morning. Jacob has gone to appraise a collection in Weatherford, Camden and Julia have the morning off, Siren Two and Ramon are late, and Sal and Heather are at the front counter, using his literary tarot cards to play a modified version of poker. Sal is not concerned about the lack of customers, however. He remembers the day not long after they opened, also a Tuesday in fact, when not a single person came in the store the entire day. The staff calls it The Day the Store Stood Still.

That will not happen today, though. In the midst of an argument over whether the Dickens card trumps the Fitzgerald, the front door opens and a young Hispanic man, maybe 22 or 23, enters. He looks intently around the store, and something about his demeanor makes Sal immediately wary. The guy looks around a few more times and then walks directly to the counter.

"Can we help you, sir?" Heather asks while trying to discreetly lay the Fitzgerald on top of the Dickens.

"I need to speak to the owner," he relies sharply.

Sal stands up from his stool, towering over the guy even with the counter between them.

"That would be me," he answers, just as sharply.

The kid takes half a step back, but recovers quickly. At the same moment, Sal sees Ramon through the front glass, but rather than coming inside – as he should – Ramon looks through the window, pauses, and then hurries away. *You just can't get good help anymore*, Sal thinks. He returns his attention to the kid, who finally speaks again.

"This is a very nice store you have," he says. "It would be a shame if something happened to it."

Heather nods, missing his meaning entirely. Sal suppresses a smile, because never in his life has he seen the opening of an attempted shakedown handled so poorly.

"Yeah, it would," Sal says. "Not likely though."

"Oh, I would not be so sure," the kid says. "It is an unpredictable world, bro."

There is something oddly familiar about this kid, but Sal can't put his finger on it. He decides to take control of the conversation.

"I'm Sal," he says, extending his hand. The kid reflexively extends his own and shakes Sal's. His palm is sweaty, Sal notices. Not a good sign.

"I am Miguel," the kid replies. "And we have business to discuss. Maybe the lady would like to go -"

"The lady isn't going anywhere," Heather answers. It appears she has picked up on the bad vibe as well. "Whatever you have to say to Sal you can say with me here."

This throws Miguel off again – he really is bad at this – and before he can recover, Sal says a single word.

"No."

Miguel doesn't appear to grasp what this means, so Sal elaborates.

"No," he repeats. "I am not giving you a single dime to ensure 'nothing bad' happens to the store. This weak-ass act may work with some around here, though I highly doubt it. I can assure you it won't work with me."

"That is a most unfortunate attitude," Miguel answers, and once again a hint of recognition tugs at Sal's mind. "We are not people who take refusal lightly."

This time Sal can't help himself; he laughs, and the kid's face falls as if Sal has just told him there's no Santa Claus.

"There is no way *you* have 'people,'" Sal says, "unless they're your kid brothers."

"You shouldn't underestimate me," Miguel says with an actual hint of menace Sal almost admires. "That'd be a big mistake."

"Perhaps," Sal replies. "And perhaps not. I'm guessing you do have some kind of weapon on you, though."

Miguel doesn't reply, but a wicked grin spreads across his face. The kid may be an amateur, but amateurs can be dangerous too.

"No jacket," Sal continues, "so the only likely options are a .22 in an ankle holster, a 9mm at the small of your back, or if you're old-school, simply a switchblade in your back pocket. Doesn't really matter, since any of the three will cover my self-defense claim."

Miguel's smile fades. He's not sure what Sal means, and before he can ask Sal has drawn a 9mm Glock from, it seems, nowhere. He levels it at Miguel's chest, his manner quite casual.

"So what do you think, Heather," he asks. "Two in the chest and one in the head? No open casket for his mama that way."

Heather's reply chills Miguel even more than Sal's gun.

"Two in the chest," she says icily. "Not mama's fault sonny turned out to be an asshole."

"W-wait," Miguel stammers. "It will be so much worse for you if you kill me."

Over Miguel's shoulder Sal sees Ortiz enter the store. He saunters toward them, unfazed by the scene he has stumbled upon. Miguel does not turn when the bell chimes; his eyes are riveted on the Glock.

"Why would it be much worse?" Sal asks. "You'd be dead. End of my problem."

"My boss will come after you," he says, his voice quivering badly now.

"I doubt you have a boss, but even if you do he's probably a fuck-up just like you. Again, no problem."

"I do have one," Miguel spits out, now visibly shaking. "His name is Luis Ortiz."

Sal did not expect this, and he shoots a quick glance at Ortiz, who neck muscles tighten. He says nothing, however.

"Yeah, I've heard of him," Sal says. "Big guy, Puerto Rican, runs with a psychotic preacher and an uppity English girl." Ortiz smiles and nods behind Miguel.

"That's him," Miguel replies. "He is your worst nightmare. He is someone you will never escape. He is -"

"Standing behind you, Miguelito," Ortiz says. Sal thinks he detects a hint of sadness in his voice.

Forgetting the gun trained on him, or perhaps wisely choosing to face the more frightening threat, Miguel spins around to face Ortiz.

"Don Luis," he says in a tone bordering on reverential. "Thank God you are here."

"You can thank God yourself, Miguel," Ortiz says sternly, "since you will be seeing him in mere moments." He looks at Sal. "I heard the last part of what the lovely

Heather said as I entered, and I concur. Do not punish his poor mother with a closed casket."

Miguel starts to cry; Ortiz stops this with a vicious backhand to his face.

"Be a man," he says. He says it as if he were asking for more coffee in a diner, and the effect is chilling.

"What will it be, Sal?" he asks. "Will you remove this nuisance, or shall I?"

Sal lowers the gun, which draws a slight nod from Luis.

"Julia gets mad when I shoot people in the store," he says. "She thinks it's bad for business."

"The lovely Camden would agree," Ortiz says. "And Heather should not have to witness such unpleasantness."

He says nothing more, makes no motion Sal can see, but immediately two men enter the store; one is thin and wiry, the other built like a tree trunk. Without a word, they guide Miguel toward the front door, the wiry one removing a switchblade from Miguel's back pocket as they go. Sal smiles at this, then thinks about where Miguel is headed, and the smile vanishes.

Later that afternoon Sal is sitting with Ortiz at a patio table outside the Dream Emporium, an untouched beer growing warm in front of him.

"You did not seem surprised when I appeared at the store this morning," Ortiz says, taking a sip of Scotch.

"I wasn't," Sal says. "When Ramon looked inside and took off without coming in I thought it was odd, especially since he was late for work. But when you showed up I understood."

"Indeed. Young Ramon recognized Miguel, whom he correctly assumed was not at the store seeking knowledge in books. He summoned me and I came immediately."

"I was surprised," Sal says, "when he mentioned your name, though not as surprised as he was when he realized you were standing behind him. What happens to him now?"

Ortiz simply shrugs, then motions to the waitress for another drink.

"Seriously," Sal persists. "Those guys who took him didn't look like altar boys."

"In fact," Ortiz says with a mischievous grin, "in their youth they actually were altar boys, much like you and I were. But clearly that is not as important to you as the fate of someone who not only tried to extort money from your beloved store, but whom you were prepared to kill in order to prevent it."

"I was defending Heather," Sal answers, with little conviction.

"Perhaps. In any case, Miguel must answer for what he has done. If it will help you sleep, let us say he has been exiled to a West Texas ghost town to serve his penance."

We could say that," Sal agrees, "though I doubt it's true. Why the ultimate penalty for a simple shakedown gone horribly, and stupidly, wrong? Especially considering the fact that he clearly idolizes you. I caught how he tried to adopt your manner of speaking."

"It is a difficult situation," Ortiz agrees.

"Camden wouldn't like it." It's the last card he can play, and he hopes he hasn't made a huge mistake playing it. Ortiz nods, but his expression remains placid.

"There is no reason for her to ever know, is there Salvatore? But if she did somehow learn of it, and protested, I would miss her."

Sal is dumbstruck.

"You'd walk away from Cam just to do away with that little shit?"

"If it came to that I would have no choice, though by then her protests could not help him. The deed is done, unless you want to hold to the ghost town idea."

"I just don't get it. It makes no sense that -" Sal stops in mid-sentence; he suddenly understands. Luis recognizes this and smiles.

"He said your name," Sal says.

"You see now."

"Yeah, I guess I do. It's not him trying to shake us down or threatening us or even being a dumbass. He identified you, stupidly thinking it would save him. If I had really been some random shopkeeper I could have given the police your name."

"He broke the code of silence," Ortiz says gravely. "That cannot be forgiven, not for you or Camden or even my brother Jake, who would have understood all of this without it being discussed. Your Family back in New Jersey would be disappointed."

"They already are," Sal says, finally taking a swig of his beer, which had grown intolerably warm. Camden would love it, the crazy Brit.

"They should not be," Luis says with a truly warm smile. "So what will you tell the lovely Camden?"

"Nothing," he says. "She worries too much as it is."

"That is quite funny," Ortiz replies, motioning to the waitress for fresh drinks. "She says the same thing about you.

19

"Every Day is Like Sunday"

"I want to go to some churches tomorrow," Saul says.

"Some churches?" Jake asks. "As in more than one?"

"Yes. I want to see the differences in the way people worship today."

"I would think you would know that already, having just come down from heaven and all."

"They weren't worshipping me, you moron," Saul says in a huff. He has picked up new insults quite quickly.

"Still," Jake protests. "You seem to know more about the 21st century than your typical 1st century 'visitor' should."

"Still skeptical, I see. I was given the information it was felt I needed. The rest I'm getting from a place called Wikipedia."

"Wonderful," Jake says as he pours them both more coffee. Saul has become addicted to the stuff. "Well, there are a lot more than we can see in one Sunday. Any in particular on your list?"

Saul takes a sip from his mug and consults a list he has made on a yellow legal pad.

"I thought we could start with the big ones, at least as far as number of adherents: Catholic, Southern Baptist, and maybe one of those Cataclysmic ones."

"Charismatic?" Jake suggests, though Saul's term isn't far off base.

"Charismatic, yes. Unfortunately there don't seem to be any Eastern Orthodox churches near here, but this is a start. Can we do three in one day?"

"That seems like a tall order," Jake says, "but let me check." He sits down at the computer and pulls up a listing of local churches and their service times, making notes on the back of a piece of junk mail advertising affordable teeth whitening.

"Oh," Saul adds, "and Methodist. There seem to be a lot of those here too."

Jake sighs and clicks to a different web page. After a few minutes he turns back to Saul.

"I think we can pull this off," he says, consulting his notes, "but we'll have to hit the Saturday night service at Briarwood. That will take care of the Southern Baptists. It starts at 6:00 p.m., so we have a couple hours to kill before we need to leave."

"Saturday night service?" Saul asks, confused. "I realize Saturday is the Sabbath, but how does that count as meeting on the first day of the week? You know, the day Jesus rose?"

"Someone somewhere decided Saturday night counts for Sunday," Jake says. "Some people work on Sunday and can't go then, some like to sleep in, and some don't want to miss the NFL pre-game shows."

"You're making this up," Saul says.

"Nope. Then tomorrow we can go to the 8 a.m. Methodist service…it's short…and still make St. Jude's for the 10:00 a.m. High Mass. You'll like that, it has incense."

"And the Charismatics?" Saul asks. "They seem very energetic."

"They are that. We can go to the 1:00 p.m. service at Pantego Pentecostal Assembly. That will give us time for lunch first."

"Lunch is important," Saul agrees. "So do I need to wear my suit tonight? I only have the one."

"No," Jake says. "Jeans are fine on Saturday night. Actually, they're pretty much okay all the time anymore."

Saul arches a bushy eyebrow at him.

"Really," Jake assures him, while thinking he should suggest trimming those eyebrows. "We've become a very casual country. In fact, you will probably see outfits that will make you want to stone someone, especially on the teenagers."

Saul remains unconvinced. "I'm going to take a nap," he announces. "Wake me when it's time to get ready."

As he leaves the room, Jake thinks to himself that Saul is no more prepared for Briarwood than Briarwood is prepared for him.

During the drive to Briarwood, Jake tries to prepare Saul for what he will see and hear tonight. He imagines that it has to be different from what Saul experienced during his lifetime, no matter how much people today like to refer to themselves as "First-Century Christians."

"It will be a little noisy when we first walk in," Jake says. "People will be chatting away, greeting friends, some making plans for what they will do later tonight. Then we'll stand and sing the first song, though midway through people will still be milling around, still talking, still coming in late and finding seats."

"That sounds very distracting," Saul says disapprovingly. "How in the world do you pray and reflect before you begin to worship?"

"We don't. We pray after the second or third song."

"Just like that? No contemplation or reflection beforehand. Just chaos, then straight into 'Let Us Pray'?"

"Pretty much," Jake answers. "Then we sing some more, do the collection, then the pastor preaches, does an altar call – that's basically a call to salvation – and then a closing prayer. It's all timed almost down to the minute.

Then it's time for lunch, or in the case of Saturday night, dinner, which is what half of the congregation is waiting for anyway."

"So you just flip a switch and go from talking about sports to talking to God to talking about food," he says.

"I guess so."

"No wonder that church is one of the biggest in America," Saul says. "Your religion has a drive-thru window."

"Drive-thru window?"

"I saw one on television."

"Right."

The sanctuary at Briarwood actually does not have a drive-thru window. It does, however, have several stained-glass windows depicting the great Baptist preachers of history, several of them still living. It is one thing Jake has never really been comfortable with; at least the Catholics wait until their saints are dead to erect graven images of them.

They sit near the back of the cavernous auditorium; Jake is careful to not take a seat that someone considers "theirs." The sanctuary has theater seats, complete with cup holders for coffee and the ability to recline. Saul glares at Jake when he leans his all the way back.

"Are you going to worship or sleep?" he asks. Jake sits up immediately.

The praise team is assembling on the platform, and the band is tuning their instruments. At exactly 6:00 p.m. the lights dim, the drummer counts four, and the sanctuary erupts with a crashing wave of sound that would not be out of place at a Metallica concert. Saul's hands fly up to cover his ears, but he lowers them after the initial shock passes.

The words to the first verse of the song appear on two enormous video screens, superimposed on a famous picture of the Old City of Jerusalem. Jake glances at Saul, who is staring intently at the picture. It occurs to Jake that while for him the picture is simply one he has grown up seeing in books and occasionally on television, for Saul this was once home, a home he has not seen for two millennia.

"You ok?" he asks, struggling to be heard over the music.

Saul nods, but does not take his eyes of the screen. When the next song begins, the background photo changes to a more generic Alpine scene. Saul lets out a soft sigh and looks around the sanctuary.

The second song ends, and the lights in the sanctuary dim. At the same moment, a spotlight shines on a large tank of water, visible through thick glass, set into the wall behind the platform. A man in a white robe stands in the water beside a small child, also dressed in a white robe. The man asks the child a few questions, and then submerges the child in the water, baptizing him with the familiar words "in the name of the Father, and of the Son, and of the Holy Spirit." When he lifts the boy out of the water, everyone applauds. Saul does not clap, but he is smiling.

His smile fades when the loud music resumes, and remains absent when the collection is taken.

"He didn't have to beg so blatantly," Saul whispers to Jake. "People should give cheerfully, not out of guilt."

He leans forward in anticipation as the pastor begins his message, but Jake knows fairly quickly that this sermon will not be to Saul's liking, assuming he understands all of it. Pastor Steve is on another of his political tirades, wrapping his displeasure with Congress in general and Democrats in particular in whatever Old Testament verses seem to fit the occasion. He gives no real application other than a veiled warning that a vote against a Republican is a vote against God.

Next comes the altar call, and people flood forward, to pray or join the church or accept Jesus as their savior. Jake knows that at least half of these were arranged ahead of time, both to make people less hesitant to come forward (no one wants to be the only one walking up in a place this size) and to make people talk later about how great the response to the call was.

Jake is about to get Saul out before the final announcements so they can beat the rush out of the parking lot when he notices the deacons carrying large silver containers to the front. He has completely forgotten that it is the night of the quarterly celebration of the Lord's Supper. He quickly explains to Saul what is happening, and though Saul seems to enjoy hearing his own words from Corinthians recited, he appears perplexed with the oyster cracker and plastic thimble of grape juice he receives.

As they drive away from Briarwood toward La Comida Mexican restaurant for dinner, Jake can tell that something is bothering Saul, but apparently he isn't ready yet to talk about it. This cannot be good.

It is not until their enchiladas arrive that Saul finally says what is on his mind. In the fashion Jake is starting to become accustomed to, he gives a summary of his thoughts before elaborating.

"Wow, you call that 'church'?" he asks as he dunks a chip in queso. "It reminds me more of a combination of a Greek play, a gladiatorial contest, and 40 lashes less one."

"That's a little harsh, don't you think?" Jake asks.

"Not at all," Saul replies. "Don't misunderstand; I'm not saying it was all bad. But it wasn't like anything I've experienced before."

"It was a straight New Testament service," Jake counters.

"Not hardly," Saul says. "The music was more of a distraction than anything. I half expected Slash to come onstage and do a solo for that last one."

"You sang songs."

"We sang *psalms*. There's a difference."

"Well, young people like upbeat music," Jake says, knowing full well that it's a weak response.

"And the message," Saul continues. "Was he teaching the Bible or holding a political rally?"

"I wondered if you would catch that," Jake says. "It's not always like that. Steve can preach a really solid message, when he wants to."

"Perhaps. And when everyone went forward, the altar call?"

"Yes. What about it?"

"There was no altar; just a stage."

"We call that the altar," Jake explains.

"An altar is a specific thing," Saul says. "That is clear in scripture."

"An actual altar is too, well, Catholic for most Baptists."

"You can't just change the meaning of words to fit what you want. You people have done that with everything it seems."

"By 'you people' I assume you mean Baptists. What else have we done it with?"

"Only two of the most important things possible," Saul exclaims, waving his fork in the air. "Baptism, first of all."

"You cannot possibly have an issue with the baptism," Jake says. "It was done exactly the way Jesus commanded it."

"I have no problem with the *way* it was done," Saul says. "However, I have a serious problem with what the pastor said about there being nothing special about the water, about it being only a symbol, an outward sign of an inward change."

"What's wrong with that?"

"Nothing special about the water?" Saul says, growing more and more animated. "If there was nothing special about baptism why would the Lord command that it be done? Read your Bible, son. Without baptism you cannot be saved; the verses that teach this are too numerous to ignore."

"Baptists don't believe that," Jake says, not adding that it is indeed something that has always bothered him.

"How ironic that the ones who call themselves Baptist are one of the only denominations to deny its sacramental nature."

Jake has no answer for this, as it is a fact. Most denominations, from Catholic to Orthodox to Presbyterian agree completely with Saul. And there is a certain irony to the name 'Baptist,' given this fact. He decides to move on to the second thing Saul believes they have changed from its original meaning.

"What's the second thing that you're bothered about?" he asks, though he has an idea even before Saul tells him.

"The Lord's Supper, as if you didn't already know. What was with the cracker and grape juice?"

"That's what we use."

"Why? Ignoring for a moment the fact that you turned that into a symbol with no real meaning as well, why in the world are you using grape juice instead of wine?"

"Because Baptists don't drink alcohol."

"You drink alcohol," Saul says, pointing at the half-empty bottle in front of Jake.

"I'm a bad Baptist. Most Baptists believe that the wine Jesus drank wasn't really wine like we know it, but water with a little wine added to kill the impurities in the water."

"Do you even hear yourself?" Saul asks, laughing so hard he sprays bits of food across the table. "Not really wine. You people do love to change words to suit you."

"Okay," Jake says. "I've never bought the idea that it wasn't really wine. But it's our tradition."

"Yet you love to point out that the traditions of men are condemned by Jesus himself."

Again Jake has no answer, and wisely doesn't try to come up with one.

"So you're saying we're wrong about everything?" Jake asks.

"Not everything," Saul says, his voice much softer now. "Definitely not everything. You get so many of the most important things right. But you have changed equally important things to fit what makes you comfortable, and that is something you simply cannot do."

Jake expects him to say more, but at that moment the waitress arrives with hot sopapillas. Saul gleefully covers several with butter and honey and then devours them, apparently forgetting their conversation entirely.

"I'm surprised you chose this place over the cathedral," Jake says as the pull up in front of St. Jude's the next morning. It's the early Mass, but the lot is still more than half full.

"This is the church where you grew up," Saul says. Jake stares at him, but then smiles and shakes his head.

"I was going to ask how you knew that," he says, "but nothing surprises me anymore. Why does that matter though?"

"Let's just say that sometimes in order to figure out where you're going, you need to go back to where you began."

"Cryptic. Very cryptic."

Jake hesitates as he reaches to open the door to the church. It has been years since he has been inside; the last time was for his father's funeral. In fact, the last three times were all funerals: his father's, his mother's, and his wife's. As if knowing what he is thinking, Saul places a reassuring hand on his shoulder and nods. Jake pulls open the door, they enter…and he is immediately seven years old again, enveloped in the lingering aroma of incense soaked into wood and marble from thousands upon thousands of Masses and face-to-face with the life-sized statue of St, Jude just inside the nave. Without even thinking, and after years as a Baptist, he reflexively dips his fingers in the font of holy water by the door and makes the sign of the cross. Saul smiles but says nothing.

Off to his left Jake sees a group of altar boys (and one altar girl) surrounding a priest. The man is of average height but solidly built, with thick salt-and-pepper hair and Clark Kent glasses. Father Boyle was wearing those glasses long before it was cool, as far back as Jake can remember. He looks up from the kids and sees Jake and Saul, a look of recognition crossing his face. He brushes past the children and makes a beeline for them.

"I honestly don't know what is more shocking," he says when he reaches them, bypassing any greeting or small talk. "Seeing Jake Donovan back at Mass or having St. Paul visit my church." With that, he bows his head to the old man – they are actually close to the same age – at which Saul places his hand on Father Boyle's head and blesses him, in Latin.

"How in the world did you know that?" Jake asks, much too loudly. "I'm still not sure I believe it."

"How can you not?" Boyle asks. Then to Saul he says "It is a great honor having you here."

They take a seat near the front at Saul's insistence, and after counting the rows of pews ahead of them Jake calculates that this would have been the row he sat in as seventh-grader at St. Jude's school. Seventh grade was when he met Lori.

Meanwhile, Saul is gazing around at everything: the stained glass windows that stretch from eye-level almost to the ceiling, twelve of them on each side of the church; the side altars with statues of Mary, St. Joseph, St. Michael the Archangel; and two large icons, one of Our Lady of Guadalupe and one of Teresa of Avila. Dominating all of it, suspended behind the high altar, is a crucifix at least ten feet tall. There is barely a sound in the huge sanctuary, and Jake notices that Saul looks as content as he has ever seen him.

After Mass, they stop for breakfast at Irma's, or as Jake calls it, the scene of the crime.

"Now that was what a church is supposed to be like," Saul says as he spoons more sugar into his coffee. "It was a sacred, beautiful space, not some sports arena."

"In the first century you met in houses," Jake replies. "Those were simple spaces."

"As if we had any choice," Saul answers. "We were not allowed to build our own churches then. And if we had been able to, if you think they would have been plain, ugly buildings then you clearly never saw the stunning beauty of the Temple in Jerusalem."

"Considering it was destroyed almost two thousand years before I was born," Jake says, "no, I never saw it."

"Fair point. But you've seen drawings, and even the disciples commented on its grandeur in the New Testament."

Jake nods; this is true.

The waitress brings their food, which halts conversation momentarily.

"You crossed yourself with holy water," Saul says when she leaves, a sly smile on his face.

"Force of habit," Jake protests. "Simply the result of thousands of times doing it before. Don't read anything into it."

"Perhaps," Saul says. "We can discuss that more later. For now, let me eat my pancakes in peace. The time I have to enjoy such things is growing short."

20

"Lay Your Hands on the Television"

Jake wakes with a start. The clock reads 3:16 am; he has only been asleep for three hours. There is a sound coming from the living room, which can only mean that Saul is watching TV. He rolls over and tries to ignore it, but knows at once it's a futile effort. He will not sleep again tonight. He pulls on shorts and a t-shirt and walks out to the living room.

Saul is perched on the edge of the couch, staring intently at the screen. He has a cup of coffee in one hand and a Pop-Tart in the other. At this hour Jake expects the show to be about miracle knives that can saw an Abrams tank in half and still cut through a tomato like it's butter or the latest home gym equipment that can make you into an Adonis in only five minutes a day for six easy installments of $99.99. But Saul is not watching an infomercial.

On the screen is a man in his sixties reclining in a large leather easy chair. He wears faded jeans, cowboy boots, and a starched white shirt with a bolo tie. On his head rests a white Panama hat with a black band. He has a white beard, though his is wispy rather than full like Saul's, and his penetrating blue eyes stare directly out at Jake as if he can actually see him.

Jake recognizes the man, of course, and not simply because he has been on television for as long as Jake has had insomnia. Jake has met him a few times, as he is broadcasting from a location less than a mile away. His hours-long monologue might indeed be mistaken for that of an infomercial huckster, but for the battered Bible on the arm of his equally battered chair. Dr. Gene Asher is a salesman, no question, but what he sells is Jesus.

"You're wasting your time watching this guy," Jake says as he takes a seat next to Saul. "He'll just make you angry like the last televangelist you saw."

"No," Saul says, his voice barely above a whisper and his eyes never leaving the screen. "This man is different. Very different."

"Different? Jake asks, surprised. "Different how?"

"This man *knows*," Saul replies. "He understands. He can communicate the truth. Sadly, he wastes his gift by going off on rants about taxes and something called the FCC and demanding money from his viewers. He only teaches for a few minutes every hour, but when he does teach..."

Jake ponders this for a moment. He has to admit that Dr. Asher has moments of clarity and brilliance, and well he should. Jake knows his background from years of watching him in the days before cable TV, back when Asher's show was the only thing on at 3 am when he could not sleep.

Gene Asher had come to Fort Worth over 30 years ago with a doctorate in New Testament Studies from the Yale Divinity School and fresh off a break with the United Church of Christ, which found his views and preaching style too radical. He purchased an abandoned Congregationalist church building on the edge of downtown long before downtown was revitalized and set about creating a media empire that would spread his version of the gospel around the world without him ever leaving the comfort of his leather armchair.

His physical congregation had grown little in the intervening years, certainly never coming close to attaining mega-church status. But his nightly viewership was in the tens of millions, as insomniacs from Boise to Boston and Brentwood to Bangor (not to mention Manila, Buenos Aires, and Dublin) tuned in nightly, eager to pledge their hard-earned money in exchange for just those nuggets of wisdom Saul had referred to. That he earned enough to buy up five hours of airtime commercial-free five nights a week was a testament to his popularity and the reach of his ministry.

"I would think he's exactly what you came here to rail against," Jake says, getting up to make himself a cup of coffee. No point in even trying to pretend he might sleep more tonight.

"He is one of the reasons I am here," Saul says. "But not to rail against. There are three I was sent here for – you people seem to think three is a magic number – and Dr. Asher is the second."

Jake is speechless. Saul was sent for Gene Asher? Then again, that was no crazier than him being sent to Jake himself.

"I assume I'm the first of the three," he says, "since you're sitting on my couch. If Dr. Gene is the second – weird, but okay – who is the third? The Pope?" The Pope is the first major religious figure who comes to mind besides Billy Graham, and why would Saul need to see Billy Graham after all?

"No, not the Pope," Saul says, laughing so hard he spills coffee on his shirt. "That's more of a job for Peter, wouldn't you think?"

"Yeah, I guess that makes sense," Jake says, not completely sure if he's serious. "Who is the third then?"

"In due time, my boy," Saul says. "Now watch; I think he's about to teach again."

Jake turns his attention back to the screen, but Dr. Asher is not quite ready to teach just yet.

"The IRS wants you to declare how much money you give me," he says, a wry smile spreading across his face. "Don't you do it! It's none of their business. It's between you, me, and God. And to show them we mean business, I want you to call the number on your screen and make a pledge. We are going to raise fifty thousand dollars before we go off the air tonight just to spite them. Get on the phone...I'll wait. Hit it boys!"

The camera swings from Dr. Asher to a group of long-haired musicians, who launch into what can only be described as a speed metal version of "The Old Rugged Cross." The camera then pans back across the room to several rows of tables with telephones and volunteers ready to take those calls, much like a charity telethon. Jake is not at all surprised to see the phones begin ringing, and soon every volunteer is speaking to one of Gene's loyal viewers. Business at The Church on the El Camino is booming.

"Trust me," Jake says, "he won't teach again tonight. I've seen this act too many times."

"A shame," Saul says with a shake of his head. "But no matter; we will go see him later today."

"He sleeps during the day," Jake says. "Like a vampire."

Saul laughs and pats Jake on the shoulder.

"He will wake for me."

To Jake's amazement, a few hours later Dr. Asher is indeed awake and they find themselves standing in the foyer of his sprawling 10,000 square foot ranch style mansion on Forest Park Dr. When Jake gives his name to the butler who answered the door – the man actually had a butler – he acts as though the old preacher is expecting him, which certainly cannot be the case. Yet here they are.

The butler leads them down a long hallway and into a library larger than Jake's entire apartment. The walls are lined with oak bookcases, the carpet is plush, and a fire crackles in the fireplace. Dr. Asher strode from behind a large maple desk on seeing Jake; he wears the same faded jeans, but now has on a loud Hawaiian shirt and flip flops.

"Good to see you again, Reverend Donovan," he says, shaking Jakes hand vigorously. "I've been watching your steady rise for years and hoped we might talk someday."

"Really?" Jake asks, perplexed. "Why?"

"I'm getting long in the tooth," Gene says with a laugh, "and I'm on the lookout for someone to help me run this thing. I wondered if you might be –"

He stops in mid-sentence, having just noticed Saul standing behind Jake. The man has a year-round tan, but all evidence of that vanishes; he is white as a sheet now. He takes a step back and actually points at Saul.

"You…," he stammers. "Why are you here? Have you come for me?"

Jake is thoroughly confused now; if he didn't know better he would swear that Dr. Asher actually recognizes Saul. He starts to say something, but Saul speaks first.

"I am indeed here for you, Eugene," Saul says in an uncharacteristically soothing tone. "But not as you fear. I am not the angel of death, but a messenger of life."

This does not seem to calm him much, and he staggers backward and drops heavily into a chair.

"Do you know who this is?" Jake asks him.

"Of course I know who it is," Gene snaps. "Don't be dense, Jake. You'd have to be blind not to recognize the Apostle Paul standing right in front of you."

"He prefers Saul," Jake says without thinking, but Saul shushes him.

"The question isn't who he is," Asher continues, "but rather why he is here."

"Search deep inside yourself," Saul tells him. "I think you know the answer."

"I don't!"

"Of course you do," Saul assures him. "You know exactly why. I am here to give you just the slightest nudge back in the right direction."

Slightest nudge? Jake thinks. This seems like a lot more than that.

"You have a superior intellect," Saul continues, "and the rare ability to turn your knowledge into wisdom that can benefit millions. You simply got off track a bit over the years."

"Off track?" Gene repeats.

"Certainly," Saul says. "Your insights, which are a gift from God, were not understood by men of lesser abilities; they told you that your vast education had made you crazy – a charge I wholeheartedly understand, having been told the same thing by a king once – and they sought to discredit you. But rather than stay true to what you know to be right, you lashed out at every form of authority you could find, from church leaders to the government. Yet the spark of your wisdom shines through all this when you actually *teach*. I am here to call you back to teaching. Stop fighting and teach."

Dr. Asher's eyes grow wide at this, and Jake expects a violent outburst like he has seen so many times on Gene's television show. He prepares to step between him and Saul, but quickly sees there is no need. Gene Asher is not angry; he is crying.

Saul walks over to where he sits and cradles Gene's head against his chest. Gene wraps both arms around him and sobs even harder; Jake feels a bit uncomfortable watching such an intimate display. After a few minutes the sobs subside and Gene is able to collect himself. Saul steps back and stands beside Jake again.

"So we understand each other then?" Saul asks.

"We do," Dr. Asher replies, giving him a single nod. "Thank you."

"Excellent. It was a pleasure meeting you, Eugene."

Without another word, and not giving Jake time to even say goodbye, Saul leads Jake from the room, down the hall, and out the door. On the short drive back to his apartment Jake finally speaks.

"That's it?" he asks. "That's all it took to put him back on the right path, as you called it?"

"Not everyone is as difficult to reach as you are, my young friend. Some need only the slightest push. Others have to be beaten over the head."

Jake ignores the jab. "So you're telling me that his show will be different from now on?"

"Everything about him will be different. Just watch tonight and see."

But Jake doesn't need to watch to know it will be true.

21

"Ramon Changes Direction"

Following the odd meeting with Gene Asher, Jake decides to stop by The Last Word to see if Heather is working and if she has time to grab a cup of coffee.

"Sorry, man," Sal tells him when he asks. "She left about 30 minutes ago with Jacob to check out a collection a guy wants to sell."

"No worries," Jake says, trying to hide his disappointment. "Just tell her I came by."

He turns to leave, but stops as Luis and his nephew Ramon enter the store together. Out of the corner of his eye he sees that Camden has noticed Ortiz' arrival as well, and he suppresses a laugh.

"Jake, my brother!" Ortiz exclaims when he sees him, "how fortuitous that you are here. Ramon and I were just discussing his future, and you may be able to give advice he needs."

Sal joins them when he hears this, as he is interested in Ramon's future as well; the young man is his hardest-working employee.

"I thought the Revolution was your future, Ramon," Sal says. You even wrote that book with your uncle." Sal is not worried that Ramon will go off and start a revolution, but he can plan all he wants while still working here.

"Alas," Luis says before Ramon can answer. "He has been drawn down a new path."

Jake is afraid to ask, but does anyway. "What new path is that, Ramon?"

"I've come to the realization that revolutionaries come and go, but Saints are forever," he says. "I've decided to become a Saint."

No one says anything for a long moment, as if waiting for him to get to the punch line, or at least elaborate. Given recent events in his life, however, Jake does take it seriously.

"Why is that?" he asks.

"Well, it's kind of a long story, but the thumbnail version is that in reading about the struggle for justice – social, economic, political – in Latin America, I stumbled across the writings of a lot of Latin American priests."

"Liberation theology?" Jake asks.

"Some of that, sure," Ramon replies with a nod. "But I was more interested in their *holiness*. Men like Oscar Romero, who died for the Faith, and Jorge Bergoglio, who stood up to corrupt politicians in Argentina while caring for the poor and leading a simple life. After that I started reading the lives of the Saints. I feel a strong affinity for St. Francis de Sales, who converted thousands of Calvinists with his piety and his pen."

"He's also the patron Saint of writers," Sal adds.

"So you're going to become a priest?" Camden hesitantly asks. Ramon laughs so hard it startles her.

"No ma'am," he says. "Not at this point at least; I still like women too much." Luis nods proudly at this. "I will finish college and then decide. I'm switching from UTA to the University of Dallas, though."

"A fine Catholic institution of learning," Ortiz says. "Much more traditional than those liberals at Notre Dame."

"You don't seem bothered by this turn of events, Luis," Sal observes.

"Not in the least, Salvatore," he replies. "There is no higher aim in life than to live as a saint – though I could never do it myself – nor any higher calling than to serve the Church, whether as a layman or clergy. Someday Ramon may be the first Puerto Rican Pope if he follows that path."

"Forgive me for saying it," Sal says, "but it surprises me that you feel that way. I had no idea you were so…devout."

Far from taking offense, Ortiz smiles broadly and his eyes twinkle. Sal thinks he hears Camden's knees buckle.

"Lou hides it well," Jake says with a laugh. "In point of fact, he hasn't missed a Sunday Mass since he was eight years old. He even made me hike 15 miles one stormy night in Bosnia, dodging snipers the whole way, to get to the nearest Catholic Church."

"Did something happen when you were eight?" Camden asks, excited to get even a glimpse into his childhood.

"I had a very high fever for several days that the doctor could not diagnose; one of the days was a Sunday, so I missed Mass. My mother feared I was on the verge of death, and she prayed fervently, asking Our Lady of Guadalupe to heal me. When I recovered she gave me this." He pulls a medallion from around his neck and shows it to them. It is silver and depicts the image of the Blessed Virgin as she appeared to Juan Diego.

"It has never left me," he explains, "and has been blessed by bishops and priests from San Juan to Philadelphia to Sarajevo. She told me I must never, ever forget that the intercession of Mary saved my life."

There is a cough from behind them when he says this, and everyone turns at the sound. A customer has walked up to them, a tall, thin, stern-faced man in his fifties. Camden starts to speak, thinking he must want help finding a book, but he speaks first.

"I couldn't help overhearing your conversation," the man says in a tone bordering on condescension, "and I feel compelled to warn you against the idolatry of worshipping Mary."

Jake suddenly recognizes him as one of the deacons from 12th Avenue Baptist. He moves to get between the man and Luis, but is too slow: Ortiz is within inches of the man's face in an instant, his hulking frame virtually blocking the skinny deacon from their view.

"I can only assume," Ortiz says with barely-controlled fury, "that in addition to being exceedingly rude you are also one of those faithful Bible-believers who somehow manages to believe only the parts of the Bible that suit you. You ignore that the New Testament clearly calls Our Lady 'full of grace,' that God chose her to be his earthly mother, that the scriptures say all generations will call her 'blessed,' that Jesus performed his first miracle at her request, that she was at the foot of the cross when all of the apostles but John had run away, and that one of the last things the Lord said from the cross was to entrust her to John's care.

"All biblical facts," he continues, barely pausing to take a breath, "not to mention the many times she has appeared since then to encourage us. She is the mother of the one you claim to follow as Savior, so you would do well to show her some *respect*."

With each point he makes, Luis has backed the man closer to the door. The man is visibly trembling, likely from a combination of fear and anger, though he is smart enough to not reply. Ortiz pushes open the door.

"Be on your way," he says sharply, "and remember what I said." The man flees, and when he returns to the group he is his usual gregarious self.

"Now what was I saying before we were so rudely interrupted?" he asks with a sweet smile. Camden lets out a sigh; Sal is almost embarrassed for her.

"You were saying you go to Mass every Sunday," Sal says, "but I've never seen you at the Cathedral." Wouldn't that be closest to where you live? In fact, where *do* you live?"

"It's like a Spanish Batcave," Jake interjects. "Even I don't know where he lives. He blindfolds me before we get there."

"Jake is a comedian," Ortiz laughs, but still does not say where he lives. "I actually attend St. Jude's in Arlington. I have known Father Boyle for many years and prefer him as my confessor."

"Hey," Sal says, "I went to confession there when I first moved down here. First time in years."

"You should go to Mass there sometime as well," Ortiz says, "and my brother Jake should return home to the Church himself."

"Return?" Sal repeats, turning to Jake. "You were Catholic?"

"Idiot," Jake says with a shake of his head. "I'm Irish, what else would I have been?"

"But you're a Baptist preacher," Sal persists.

"A long story for another time," Jake says, shutting down any more questioning.

"So, Luis," Camden says, "does this mean that I would have to convert for us to keep seeing each other?" She tries to make it sound like she's joking with him, but her voice quavers just a bit.

Ortiz doesn't answer immediately, and as he heads for the door it appears he may not answer at all. But he stops at the door and turns back to her.

"No need to convert, lovely Camden," he says. "Just know that our children will be raised in the One True Faith." And with that, he is gone.

22

"The Apostle and the Booksellers"

"I can't believe the Apostle Paul is in our bookstore," Jacob gushes.

"And I can't believe you've bought into the old guy's story so easily," Sal says. "I haven't seen you this excited since that Russian tourist told you we have the best collection of Russian authors this side of Moscow."

Sal had been sure that Jacob would be the most skeptical when Jake had explained that Saul was not his uncle, but instead was the Apostle Paul returned in the flesh to deliver a message about God knows what, no pun intended. Jacob was a solid "frozen chosen" Presbyterian who liked his religion very black and white. This situation was as far from black and white as you could get.

"He proved it to me," Jacob whispers. "Out of respect for my age and piety."

"Piety? You're the least pious person I know. Pompous, yes, but not pious."

"Scoff if you want, but I am now the only person on earth who knows what Paul's 'thorn in the flesh' was. I can't tell anyone, of course, since he swore me to secrecy. He said it felt good to finally tell someone though."

"I have no idea what you're talking about," Sal says, "except that you are a thorn in my side."

"Don't you read the Bible?" he asks. "I thought the nun had scared you into doing that at least."

"I read the Gospels sometimes," Sal says. "And the history parts of the Old Testament. Those are exciting. The parts about rules and lists of who begat who put me to sleep."

"You're going to have to do better than that if you have any long-term plans with Julia. She's a Baptist, and this stuff matters to her."

"I think she picks and chooses what matters to her, just like everyone else does," Sal says sharply. He immediately feels bad about this. "What I mean is, if she was a serious Bible thumper, would she be with me? Not very likely."

"People are complex," Jacob replies. "Like Russian nesting dolls."

"Russian nesting dolls, thorns in sides, I think I liked it better when you just refused to speak to me."

"Just read Second Corinthians, chapter 12," Jacob says. "You'll get it." He laughs, slaps Sal hard on the back, and walks over to assist a customer who has wandered into the rare book room.

Sal looks over at the religion section where Ortiz, who has appeared from nowhere, is in deep conversation with Jake and Saul. He moves close enough to hear what they are saying, but doesn't join in immediately.

"I believe we could use the arrival of the great Apostle both to spread the word and increase our income," Ortiz says. "It would have to be handled with the utmost tact and respect, of course."

"We are not going to sell tickets for people to watch him parade around like a trained pony," Jake says. "Or whatever it is you have in mind."

"I am hurt that you would think me capable of something so crass," Ortiz says, almost managing to look hurt. "I was thinking perhaps a series of lectures and a modest fee for such a rare opportunity."

"I'm sorry, Luis," Saul says, giving him a pat on the shoulder. "I never charged for my message in life, and I'm certainly not going to charge for it in…well, in whatever this is." He notices Sal and beckons him over.

"Jake tells me you expanded the religion section," Saul says. "How is that working out?"

"Not very well, to be honest with you," Sal admits. "Like Heather said the first day you came in here, most people like to buy their Bibles and religious books from a Christian bookstore. They love us for literature and crime novels and your basic secular reading material, but not the spiritual stuff."

"What I don't understand is why there are separate bookstores selling very different items, yet they all claim to follow Christ," Saul says, shaking his head. "Why is St. Iraneus Books so different from Damascus Road Christian Superstore?" There is a note of distaste in his voice when he says 'Damascus Road Christian Superstore.'

"It's a denominational thing," Jake says. "We've discussed this."

"Well it's just plain wrong," Saul says. "Jesus did not pray that we would be many; He prayed that we would be one. It would be nice to see those stores combined, with less of the obvious commercialism we saw at Damascus Road. Maybe even add a few things from the other world religions. Buddha had some good sayings; I even stole a few of them."

"Never going to happen," Jake says. "But it's a nice idea."

Sal, however, has the beginning of an idea, and when he looks at Ortiz, he can tell Luis is having the same thought. Neither of them says anything, however, and Saul moves on to another subject.

"I am tired of reading nothing but commentaries," he announces. "Can one of you fine booksellers recommend a good novel?"

In an instant he is besieged with suggestions.

"Bulgakov's *The Master and the Margarita*," Jacob shouts as he rushes back over to where the group is standing.

"*The Old Man and the Sea,*" says Heather from directly behind Sal; he had not even known she was there. "It's short but amazing."

"Asimov," comes Ben's voice from deep in the store. "Anything by Asimov."

Saul seems overwhelmed, trying to listen to everyone speaking at once. Sal walks over to a table near the counter and picks up a thick trade paperback. He returns to the group and places the book in Saul's hand.

"*The Shadow of the Wind* by Carlos Ruiz Zafon," he says. "It is excellent, just don't start it at night or you may stay up until morning reading it." He looks at the staff and smiles. "That's what is called 'hand selling' children. You need to get better at it before my store goes bankrupt."

"Are you quite certain that a gothic novel is the best choice for a saint?" Jacob asks. "Perhaps some Chesterton or Tolkien instead."

"No," Sal says firmly. "Zafon is what he needs. If I knew he was going to be here long enough I would suggest the *Spenser* series, but it would be a shame to start and not be able to finish all the books."

"This book sounds fine," Saul says as he reads the back cover. "It says here that every book has a soul. That's a sentiment I can agree with."

No one can argue this point, and Saul and Jake leave the store. Sal immediately rushes to the counter and pulls out a small note card; at the top is printed "Staff Picks." He scribbles something on the card, and then walks over to the table where he got the book and tapes the card to the table in front of the remaining pile of Zafons. When he has moved away the rest of them lean down to read it. It says: "If it's good enough for the Apostle Paul, then it's good enough for you. Just buy it."

23

"The New Store"

"How many Bibles did we sell today, Sal?" Camden asks as they are closing up the shop on what was a very slow day.

"None," he says cheerfully.

She stares at him for a minute, having expected her question to start a fight; she knows that they have not sold a single one since he reorganized the religion section.

"You certainly don't seem bothered by it," she says.

"I'm not. In fact, I'll be putting it all back the way it was after everyone leaves. Julia and Ramon are going to help me."

She nods, though she is still shocked both at how easily has admitted defeat and how well he is taking it. This is not like Sal at all.

"So you realized the religious book market isn't for you, I see."

He looks up from the deposit slip he is filling out and gives her a mischievous smile, the one that never bodes well for her.

"Not in the least, cousin," he replies. "Not in the least."

"But you just said –,"

He raises a hand to stop her.

"All will be revealed in the fullness of time," he says. And though she peppers him with more questions, he will not say another word on the matter.

Over the next several days Camden continually attempts to find out what Sal is up to. The worst part is that everyone seems to know but her; Julia is clearly involved, as are Ramon and Heather. Yet no one will tell her anything. She is nearly at her wits' end one morning when Father Boyle, Sister Mary Louise, Jake, and Ortiz enter the store. The sight of these four together is enough to briefly drive Sal's plan from her mind. But when Sal appears from upstairs wearing a suit, she suddenly grasps that they are part of his scheme as well.

Sal strides past her without a word, shaking the three men's hands and nodding a hesitant greeting at the nun while keeping Father Boyle between them.

"Will the Bishop be there?" he asks excitedly.

"Yes," Father Boyle replies. "His Eminence will meet us for the ribbon-cutting at 11:00 am.

Sal nods and turns to Jake.

"And the ministers?" he asks, a little more doubtfully.

"I managed to get the pastors of First Methodist, First Presbyterian, and St. Cyril's Greek Orthodox," he replies. "The Baptists all said no, and the Pentecostals never replied."

"That's okay," Sal says. "You can represent the Baptists."

"No one person can ever represent the Baptists," Jake says with a laugh, "but I'll do my best."

"Would someone please tell me what is going on here?" Camden exclaims, refraining from using a few choice expletives only because of the presence of the clergy.

"No time now," Sal says curtly. "The reporters will arrive soon and we need to be there. I don't think Ramon is ready to handle that yet, even with Julia there."

"Even with her where?" Camden asks, even more confused. "Julia is off today, and Ramon's not due in until 3:00."

"Look," Sal says, his tone even sharper now, "I can either explain when I get back or you can come along. But we have to get going."

With that he rushes out the door, the others following close behind. After a brief hesitation, Camden makes a decision.

"Jacob!" she calls across the room. "I'll be back in a little while. Ben is here if you get swamped." She hurries after them without waiting to hear Jacob's answer.

She had expected to see them getting into cars, but instead they are walking up Goliad at a brisk pace; she can see that Ortiz is talking with the nun and Sal is gesturing wildly as he speaks to Father Boyle. She considers running to catch up, but will not give Sal the satisfaction. She simply matches their pace to make sure they don't lose her.

There is no chance of that, however, as the group stops about fifty yards ahead of her and enter a storefront. She recognizes it as the former location of a New Age bookstore and smoothie bar that went out of business only a few months after opening. As she draws even with where Sal had entered, she can read the lettering on the front plate glass window: "Emmaus Books and Coffee." Under the name, in an antique script, is a single line: "We have what your soul needs" and under that a verse: John 17:20-21.

Camden is about to open the front door when Sal bounds out, nearly colliding with her. He holds a long strand of wide red ribbon in one hand and a roll of duct tape in the other. Without even acknowledging her presence, he tapes one end of the ribbon to the door frame, about chest high. He lets the other end drop straight down from there, then turns and finally speaks.

"I'll tape the other end on when we're all outside and the Bishop's here," he says, as if this explains everything.

"What –?" she stammers.

Sal takes her by the arm and leads her to the door.

"I have a couple minutes," he says as the step inside. "Let me tell you a story."

Sal's story, compelling as it may be, has to wait for Camden to recover from what she sees once they are inside. She is frozen in place as she gazes around and what she knows was the detritus of the former occupant mere weeks before; she knows because she glanced inside as she was walking past one evening. There has been an astounding transformation since then. Now, in this surreal moment, she sees a fully-functioning bookstore, but one much different than any bookstore she has seen before.

The previous occupant had suffered from a lack of start-up funds, and as a result had left the original battleship-gray paint untouched, as well as the inadequate overhead lighting; this had surely hastened their demise, since New Age adherents like bright colors. Now, however, the walls are a soft, warm shade of brown, which while still not neon-bright fit the oak bookcases perfectly; the bookcases themselves are a significant upgrade over the white IKEA shelves that were in place before. The lighting has also been upgraded significantly; the combination of overhead and recessed lights virtually mirrors that used at The Last Word.

The actual layout of the place, however, is nothing like her store. It is essentially split in half by the smoothie bar from the old store, which sits exactly in the center of the space and has been retained and converted into a coffee bar. The chrome of the espresso machines gleams brightly, and she imagines they must have cost a fortune. A young woman she does not recognize is busily brewing lattes.

There are small tables on both sides of the oval coffee bar. Ramon sits at one of them looking both confident and terrified at the same time; his suit is a carbon-copy of the one Sal is wearing. Julia is off to the left, organizing a bookshelf.

The books seem to all have religious themes, and toward the back on the right side Camden can see a shelf containing small statues, one of which she immediately recognizes as Mary. She wanders to the left side of the store and notes that there is a much larger variety of Bibles on this side than on the right. She finally turns to Sal.

"What is all this?" she asks.

"It's my answer to there being no Christian bookstore downtown," he says. "You knew when I reorganized the section in our store that it wouldn't work, and you were right. I saw that pretty quickly, but didn't want to admit it."

"Say that again," she says.

"You were right," he says with a laugh.

"But that doesn't explain all this," she says, gesturing around the store with her arm.

"This is the result of a comment by Jake's friend the saint and a chance meeting with Luis at Billy McGee's bar.

We talked about what Saul said, and about this new direction Ramon is taking, and agreed that he can't be a stock boy forever. By the fourth beer we had determined that we should open a new kind of religious bookstore and that Ramon should run it. Ramon thinks it's a great idea."

"A new kind of religious bookstore?" Camden repeats. "New how?"

"Come with me," Sal says, taking her by the arm, "and see if you notice anything different about this one. I know it will be difficult for your completely secular British mind, but try."

He leads her first to the left side of the store. She sees the large assortment of Bibles more closely now, noting that there are numerous translations, including the King James, the New International Version, the New Millennium Reader's Version, and the Holman Christian Standard Bible, or HCSB. She picks up one of these and looks at it.

"Jake calls the HCSB the Hard Core Southern Baptist Bible," Sal says with a laugh.

She nods, though she barely hears him. She is overwhelmed by the different types of Bibles on offer here: children's Bibles, student Bibles, Bibles with John Wesley's sermons as study notes, Bibles for people from the Anglican, Presbyterian, and even Orthodox traditions. The Orthodox Study Bible has a beautiful icon on the cover. There are also The Busy Mom's Devotional Bible, the Fireman's Bible, and the Life Recovery Bible.

He pulls her farther along and she sees shelf after shelf of books on missions, on prayer, and on evangelism; there are also more commentaries on the Bible than she has ever seen before (not that she's seen many before).

"Let's move to the other side," he says, ushering her past a music and video section and what looks like a clothing section with a lot of T-shirts with religious themes.

They are at the back of the right side of the store now, and she can see the statues on the shelves more closely. She was right about one being the Virgin Mary, but it turns out that several different ones are as well, each with a small tag attached: Our Lady of Lourdes, Our Lady of Guadalupe (lots of those), and Our Lady of Grace. There are also small statues of the apostles and many of saints she's never heard of. One entire shelf contains nothing but crucifixes.

As they move closer to the front there are more commentaries, as well as books on apologetics, the saints, the sacraments, and the history of the Catholic Church. There are Bibles as well, though far fewer variations. There seem to be only three translations (the Revised Standard Version, The New American Bible, and the Douay-Reims), and the only specialty versions (Sal's words) consist of children's, teen's and the Ignatius Study Bible (New Testament Only). Along the wall at the front are pictures of the Pope (both John Paul II and Benedict XVI), cards with saints' pictures, rosaries, and some truly beautiful artwork.

Sal takes a seat at one of the empty tables and gestures for Camden to join him. He is smiling like a kid at Christmas; clearly his expects that she gets it now. She does not.

"I don't get it," she says, barely masking her frustration. "It's just a religious bookstore like any other."

"You have got to be kidding," he says, not masking his frustration at all. "There has never been a Christian store like this anywhere. It carries books, Bibles, art, you name it, from *all* of the different denominations. St. Iraneus Bookstore would never carry Protestant versions on the Bible, and Damascus Road Books would close before stocking a picture of a saint."

Her eyes widen, and she looks around the store again as if seeing it for the first time. But just as quickly they narrow, and her expression becomes hard.

"Catholic on one side," she says coldly, "and Protestant on the other, with a buffer zone in between. It *has* been done Sal."

"What? Where?"

"Northern Ireland," she replies. "Do we really need a bookstore version of the war between the IRA and the Ulster Defense Force?"

Sal is speechless for a long moment. He had not considered this, but being that she is British it should not surprise him that the Troubles that raged for 30 years would elicit such a response. He thinks hard before answering.

"I can see where that might be your initial reaction," he says in a low voice. "But this is actually just the opposite. This place is meant to bring all of those disparate views together under one roof, to show each group that the "other" isn't some kind of demon. That's why we chose the verse on the front window, the one where Jesus prayed that his followers would all be one."

"And how exactly does this place achieve that?" she asks, unconvinced. "Even here you have the Protestants and the Catholics separated."

"The store acknowledges the separation," he says. "It would be a lie to act like that doesn't exist. But we have come up with ways to bring the two sides together. Jake says there are actually a lot more than two sides – Protestant vs. Catholic, Catholic vs. Orthodox, Baptist vs. Methodist – but we had to start somewhere."

"What ways?"

"Notice the tables at the front of the store," he says, pointing at two large tables just inside the entrance. "Those are the books from both the Evangelical and Catholic current best-sellers' list, and they're all mixed in together. People looking for Beth Moore's latest book on Christian living will be rubbing shoulders with, and hopefully talking to, the guy looking for Benedict XVI's latest book on Jesus."

She nods slightly but does not speak.

"Also," he continues, "we put things like Billy Graham's autobiography in the saints section, Pope John

Paul II's books on the family in the Christian living section, stuff like that. You have to cross over to get what you're looking for."

Silence.

"And it's not just Christian stuff. We have the Vedas, Upanishads, Sufi poetry, and Korans. Ramon wants a variety of viewpoints in the discussion."

A raised eyebrow and more silence.

"The coffee bar is set up to encourage mingling," he says. "In fact, if you order on one side you have to pick up your drink on the other. There will also be speakers from all traditions giving talks at night, like a spiritual poetry slam."

She finally laughs at this last part.

"It is a bold idea," she admits, "though I'm still not sure it will work. The real question is when did you become so interested in spiritual unity?"

"Actually," he says, the mischievous grin returning, "I don't care about that at all; most of these ideas came from Jake and Ramon. You know me; my religion is books, and this is just one step in my quest to turn Fort Worth into a true book town."

"That makes more sense," she replies. "Though I notice there isn't much fiction."

"Christian fiction is mostly crap," he says. "We've discussed this before. Though there is a wide selection of Amish Romance; it's very popular with the Charismatics."

"Amish Romance?"

"No sex," he explains. "Just 300 pages of bonnets and longing looks."

"Right. I still don't see how you got all of this done in such a short time."

"That was the easy part," Sal says. "Luis loves his nephew, and you would be amazed how quickly things happen when you pay in cash. Ramon and his friends did a lot of the interior work – painting, staining shelves, stuff like that – and well-paid contractors did the rest. I mainly advised and consulted, ordered what Jake and Father Boyle suggested, and stayed out of the way. I'm more of a silent partner."

"I see," Camden says. "And what is your next grand plan to transform downtown?"

"I'm thinking Ben may need his own Sci-Fi and comic book store," he says without hesitation. "He –"

"Absolutely not," she says firmly. "You can scheme all you want, but no more taking away our employees."

He is about to reply when the Bishop of Fort Worth walks in. Sal rises quickly to greet him, thanking him profusely for coming out to cut the ribbon and bless the new store.

"It's the least I can do to foster ecumenical relations in our city," the Bishop replies, "especially after your recent donation of the statues of St. Francis de Sales and St. John of the Cross to our cathedral. Most generous."

This "donation" had only occurred after Sister Mary Louise shamed Sal into stopping his plan to turn The Last Word into a tax-exempt church. She is standing to the side of the bishop, and Sal glares at her. She smiles sweetly back at him, content that she continues to have the upper hand.

24

"God and Mammon"

If Jake's office at Briarwood was impressive, Senior Pastor Stephen Campbell's office makes Jake's look like the cupboard under the stairs where Harry Potter spent his first eleven years. It is easily three times as big and has, of all things, a working gas-log fireplace. There are two floor-to-ceiling oak bookcases (Jake has only one), a mahogany desk you could land an F-16 on, and even a separate room with couches and a wall-mounted flat-screen television. Being the big boss of one of the biggest churches in the world has its perks.

Jake and Saul are ushered into the room by Steve's personal secretary, a male seminary student. Steve avoids even the hint of impropriety by refusing to have a female secretary; it has engendered both admiration and jokes over the years. Once they are seated across from the pastor, the young man hurries away to get them all beverages: water for Steve, Dr Pepper for Jake, and, of course, coffee for Saul.

Stephen leans back in his chair and regards the older man sitting next to Jake. He is quite curious as to why Jake was so insistent that they meet, and why he would give no details prior to their arrival. However, he is used to Jake's quirks, and is sure it's nothing all that serious.

"So what did you want to talk about, Jake?" Stephen asks once they all have their drinks.

"It's sort of a long story, Steve," Jake replies, "and a little hard to believe. But I would ask that you hear me out." Jake still feels weird calling him by his first name, but Steve hates being called Doctor, even though he holds both PhD and Doctor of Divinity degrees.

"Have I ever not heard you out, my friend?" Stephen asks with a smile. "And I have taken your side several times when no one else would. Spill it."

This was true. In spite of his semi-celebrity within the evangelical world, there were a number of high profile members who simply did not like Jake. Maybe it was because he had killed people for a living before being called to the ministry, though he doubted that. This was Texas, and shooting people barely qualified as a misdemeanor here, let alone a sin.

"Okay," Jake says. "This gentleman's name is Saul, and we met a few weeks ago."

"Yes," Stephen says. "I think I saw him at the Saturday night service."

"He wanted to see what worship was like at Briarwood."

"And did you enjoy it, sir?" he asks Saul.

"It was not what I am used to," Saul answers diplomatically.

"The thing is," Jake continues, "Saul has some suggestions he would like us to consider."

"Suggestions?" Stephen repeats. "This is sounding a little unusual Jake. You know how things work here. Members go to the deacons or Sunday school leader if they have ideas, and those are brought to us. This man isn't even a member yet."

"I need no membership in your congregation to speak my mind," Saul says sternly. "And I have not brought suggestions. I have brought a message from the Lord."

Steve looks at Jake, who shrugs.

"I told you his name was Saul," he says. "It's also Paul. Tell the pastor where you're from."

"I am originally from Tarsus," he says. "Most recently I resided in the presence of the Lord Jesus."

"You're saying that you are the Apostle Paul?" Steve says. "Jake, have you lost your mind?" He starts to stand but Saul leaps to his feet first.

"I am who I say that I am," he says in voice much deeper than normal. "And the one I say sent me did send me. Will you hear the message?"

"I think you need professional help, sir," Steve says. "It would be better if you heard from a doctor."

This is a mistake. Saul seems to grow in size, and the area around him darkens, just like Gandalf when Bilbo accused him of trying to steal the One Ring. His voice sounds like Gandalf's now as well.

"Do not speak to me as if I am a child, Stephen Paul Campbell," Saul booms. "You have proven yourself unworthy of either of those names. You have been granted a position of great responsibility and yet abuse it daily. You put on a show of fidelity by having a male secretary while doing much more than coveting your next door neighbor's wife. You use my words to preach division and malice while claiming to love the sinner but hate his sin. You build monuments to yourself in the form of church buildings while people created by the God you claim to serve starve in their very shadows. You have been tested and found wanting, but you have one chance to turn from this path. Will you take it?"

Both Stephen and Jake are stunned into silence by this outburst. For the first time since he and Ortiz were pinned down by enemy fire outside of Mogadishu, Jake is afraid. Stephen initially looks as if he is about to cry, but amazingly his face reverts to normal almost immediately.

"That was quite a tirade," he says, his voice as even as if he was giving the invitation at the end of a service. "What exactly do you think I need to do to turn from my supposedly wrong path?"

"Before you can do anything else you must realize how far you have fallen," Saul says, both his voice and size somehow normal again. "Repent and remember the things you did in the beginning. Return to your first love."

"You're quoting Revelation to me?" Steve says with a laugh. "I would think that an Apostle could do better."

Jake expects another explosion for Saul over this flippant response, but the old man surprises him.

"Perhaps a few reminders would convince you." Saul says in a voice so soft he has to strain to hear. Steve leans forward across his desk, trying to hear as well. "There was the time in Durant when your congregation numbered less than 50 and your salary barely fed you and your wife and small daughter. Yet you still shared what you had with the migrant worker who appeared at your door one winter night."

Steve lets out a gasp, but before he can speak Saul continues.

"Or the time when your son had a high fever and you lacked the money for medicine," he says. "You cried out to the Lord for help, a true and honest cry, and before the deacon arrived minutes later, unbidden, with a check someone had sent to the church for you, the fever had gone."

Steve doesn't even attempt to respond to this; he is now leaning all the way across his desk. Jake is quite simply frozen in place.

"Or the time," Saul says, "the one time, when you turned down a call to a larger church because you knew the work you were doing in Lufkin was what you were supposed to be doing. But then an even bigger offer came, and you have chased the bigger offers all the way here."

Steve slumps back in his chair; he looks physically and emotionally drained.

"There is no way you could know any of that," he whispers. "Only my wife knew about the migrant worker, and no one ever knew about my prayer during Adam's illness."

"God knew," Saul says. "And in order for me to reach you, he allowed me to know."

"So if you really are the Apostle Paul -" Steve says.

"He prefers Saul," Jake says, finding his voice.

"I actually wish Slash had been an option when I was alive," Saul says. "It has a manly ring to it."

"Right," Steve says, shooting a quizzical glance at Jake. "If you really are Saul, what exactly do you want from me?"

"Abandon this mercenary road you are on, stop raising millions to build your own little kingdom in the name of one who had nowhere to lay his head, and use your position to change the direction of what you erroneously call Christianity."

Jake expects Steve to instantly agree; given what Saul has just revealed about him how could he do otherwise? But amazingly Steve's expression hardens.

"I will do no such thing," he says. "I do not know what demon from the pit has told you these things about my past, but I can assure you that I am doing the Lord's work and will not be turned from it."

"But Steve," Jake says, "how can you ignore this man?"

"This man is clearly unstable at best, Jake," he replies, his normal calm now fully returned, "and possessed by a demon at worst. As for you, my friend, I have always worried about your somewhat liberal, almost Communist leanings."

"Steve -" Jake persists, but is cut off.

"This meeting is over," Steve says, pressing a button on his phone. The young assistant hurries in. "Please escort these gentlemen out of the building," he says. "But first allow Pastor Donovan to gather whatever he needs from his office. He is taking a leave of absence."

Jake is still fuming as he pulls his truck, now packed with his belongings from what will, after a vote of the deacons, no longer be his office, out of the Briarwood parking lot. Saul is silent, which seriously annoys Jake.

"Don't you have anything to say?" he snaps. "You basically just got me fired."

Saul stares hard at him for a long time; Jake is suddenly afraid he's going to go all Angry-Gandalf on him. Instead, a smile slowly spreads across his face.

"You should thank me," Saul replies.

"Thank you? I should toss you out my truck right now."

"You won't, not that you could even if you tried. I'm tougher than I look." Saul burst out laughing, clearly finding this much more amusing than Jake does.

25

"Saul Explains Himself (Sort of)"

Early that same evening, Saul is drinking his umpteenth cup of coffee and watching a *Seinfeld* rerun when Sal picks up the remote and switches off the television.

"Hey!" Saul yells. "Turn that back on."

"Nope," Jake replies, stepping back as Saul grabs for the remote. "I have some questions for you, and this time you're going to answer me."

"But it was almost over," he protests. "How will I know if they ever got a table in the Chinese restaurant?"

Jake sighs, turns the TV back on, presses "record," then turns it off again.

"You can watch the end after we're done."

Saul nods grudgingly and leans forward on the couch.

"So what questions do you have, as if I don't already know?"

"Of course you know!" Jake replies. "I've been trying to get answers from you since you got here, which has been quite a while, by the way. You have managed to turn my life upside down, and for what reason? Why am I so important that you come here after being dead – sorry – for 2,000 years? Hell, you told Sal what he needed to do the first day you met him."

Saul stares at him in disbelief, then bursts out laughing. This is becoming too common a reaction for Jake's liking, and he is not amused.

"Ok," Saul says, regaining his composure, "I'm not sure exactly where to start, since everything you just said is completely wrong."

"What? How?"

"I did not tell Sal what he needed to do, like it was some mission from God or something. I simply put an idea in his head, and even then it took some luck for him to run with it."

"So telling him to start a book town isn't part of the reason you're here?" Jake asks.

"Not at all. Like I told you before, I have a fair amount of knowledge about the people around you; it makes my job easier. I know, therefore, that Sal needs a goal, or more correctly a scheme, to be working on all the time. If not, he gets bored and starts planning grand museum heists and armed robberies and such. Not good. I simply put the idea of a book town in his head to keep him occupied for a while. It won't last."

"So, it was just a coincidence that you stumbled upon him looking for me?"

"Basically, though I would have given him the nudge at some point regardless. He was moving into dangerous territory and no one seemed to notice."

"Really? How so?"

"Apparently, and do not ask how I know this because I'm not sure myself, he had been visiting the Sid Richardson Museum every day for weeks before I arrived. They have an exhibit that includes a jewel-encrusted Bible owned by Catherine the Great. Sal wants it."

"Ah," Jake says. "That is bad."

"Moving on to your second grossly inaccurate assumption," Saul says, "this is most certainly not the first time in 2,000 years that I have been back on earth, though it is the latest period in history I've come to."

"It's not?" Jake is shocked to hear this.

"Of course not. Surely you're not so arrogant as to think you are the first person anyone has visited?"

"Well no, I guess not," Jake replies sheepishly. "Wait. You said 'anyone.' Does that mean others have come back besides you?"

"Yes, others have come back, sometimes successfully and sometimes with disastrous results. Matching personalities is important."

"Give me an example." Jake's head is spinning now. All he wanted was some answers.

"Martin Luther," Saul says.

"Martin Luther? Reformation Martin Luther? Who was he sent to?"

"No, no," Saul says. "Someone was sent to him. In fact, he was sent the Apostle Peter himself in an effort to stop the Reformation, and the horrible split among Christians, before it ever happened. Unfortunately, two bullheaded idiots are far worse than just one, and Luther not only ignored Peter's warnings but essentially cut him out of his theology from that point on."

"This seems a tad far-fetched," Jake says. "Luther was a giant of the church."

"Luther was a moron. The only reason he became a priest was because he got scared during a lightning storm, hid under a tree – not smart – and promised Saint Anne – or Saint Monica, I can't remember – that if he survived he would become a monk. Better for the world if he had become a lawyer like his father wanted."

"So, Peter failed."

"Yes," Saul says. "But he took his revenge in 1901 by helping start the Pentecostal Movement. Luther would have hated that."

"Would have? Don't you know for sure since you still see him?"

"Luther is not in the same place I am. Not by a long shot. He had the chance to reform the Church, and instead he splintered it."

His tone convinces Jake it's time to move on from this subject.

"I'm not the first, then" he says, a little sullenly. "But clearly I'm supposed to do something significant or you wouldn't be here."

"Perhaps. Or it could be that you're supposed to *not* do something. Remember what I just said about Peter and Luther. He needed to stop, and didn't."

"What am I doing that I shouldn't be, then?" he asks, more confused than ever. "I would understand if you were trying to get Ortiz to stop any number of things he does every day, but me?"

Saul smiles at this.

"Luis Ortiz falls into an entirely different category," he says. "I could never sway him, in any way, in a million years. In fact, I have next to no insight into him at all."

"How is that possible?" Jake asks. "You seem to know a lot about all of us."

"Ortiz is unique," Saul says, searching for the right way to explain. "Look at it this way. You know how God says in the Torah that we are not to put any other gods before him?"

"Sure."

"Notice that he doesn't say there *are* no other gods; he specifically says to put him above them all."

"So?" Jake has no clue where he's going with this.

"That implies that there are other gods. Lord knows the Israelites chased plenty of them. Same with the Greeks, Romans, Norse, Chinese, Indians, Native Peoples, you name it."

"You're saying there really are a bunch of other gods out there?"

"Indeed," Paul replies. "Over time, you developed, as modern Christians, the idea that they weren't real, but were rather anything placed ahead of God, *the* God. You decided that "gods" meant money or power or possessions, anything placed ahead of God. Not true. There really are gods, goddesses, demi-gods, demons, and so forth, all still running around, some doing good and some causing mischief. This despite your best efforts to eradicate, ignore, or assimilate them."

Jake stares hard at Saul, yet again trying to decide if he is serious. It appears he is.

"Assuming this is all true," he says, "and I'm not saying I agree, but assuming it is, what does it have to do with Ortiz?"

"Simple. It's entirely possible that Ortiz is a god."

Jake is speechless for a long while, waiting for Saul to laugh at his obvious joke. He does not.

"Ortiz is not a god," Jake says finally. "He may think highly of himself, and will occasionally say things like 'I ran like a god today,' but even he would be offended by the very thought. In his own particular, when-it's-convenient way, he is actually a very devout Catholic."

"You think gods can't be devout toward higher powers? You think Apollo didn't bow before Zeus?"

"Ortiz is not a god!" He is yelling now, but Saul is totally calm.

"Were you there when he was born?" Saul asks. The question catches him by surprise.

"No, of course not. We met in basic training."

"Is he larger than life? Does he recover miraculously quickly from injury? Can he do things that defy 'normal' explanation?"

"Yes, yes, and yes," Jake replies. "And that proves nothing."

"Jake, you know as well as I do that you can never prove or disprove the existence of God, or a god. You simply gather as much evidence as you can and take the rest on faith. The evidence for Ortiz is there; the faith part never can be because you are too close to him to make that kind of transition."

"If Ortiz was a god he would have told me. He would tell *everyone*."

"Of course he's not a god," Saul says with a mischievous smile. "I said all that stuff because I love watching you get worked up, and I don't have much time left to mess with you. Enough digression, though."

"Yes, back to the important part. What the hell is your job with me?"

Saul signs dramatically, but there is a gleam in his eye.

"It's simple, really," he says. "I have to put you on a new path before you cause a global conflagration."

"Seriously?" Several scenarios flash through Jake's mind, each increasingly more cataclysmic.

"Well, probably not a conflagration," Saul concedes. "But it's definitely time for you to move on to something new. Think about it a while, and you'll see that I'm right. Can we watch the end of Seinfeld now?"

"No, we cannot." You can't just end on 'conflagration.' What do you mean I need to move on to something new?"

Saul sighs heavily and glances at the darkened screen of the television.

"You have to stop preaching," he says finally. "I know it, and you know it."

"What?" Jake asks, stunned. "You tell Dr. Gene and Stephen to preach better, differently, whatever, but me you tell to stop altogether?"

"Yes. Shall I point out some reasons that should be obvious?"

"I think you should, yes."

"Fine," Saul says, settling back on the couch. "Let me ask a few questions, and I want you to be honest with yourself when you answer." If your wife had not died so tragically young would you be preaching now?" Would you even be a Protestant at all?"

Jake doesn't even need to ponder that one.

"No," he says. Lori was as Catholic as they come. She would have killed me."

"Had you not found that Bible study group at Fort Lewis after feeling so guilty about going nearly insane after her death and doing so many stupid things, would you still be preaching now?"

"Probably not."

"Had you not discovered you have a gift for reaching and persuading people, convincing them of the rightness of your point of view, would you be preaching now?"

"Maybe." He does like how this is going.

"Isn't your favorite part about mission work traveling overseas like you did in the military?"

Jake has to think that one over for a bit before answering.

"Yeah, I guess it is." *Damn it.*

"Finally," Saul says, "and this is an odd question to ask, but don't you miss killing people?"

This last question shocks Jake more than anything Saul has said since he arrived. The implication of it is staggering.

"Are you telling me I'm *supposed* to be killing people? That that's my mission in life?"

Saul shakes his head quickly.

"It's not as simple as that, son," he says. "But you, and more specifically you and Ortiz, have a special skill that is valuable in the world. You have an ability to do things and go places that others would never dare, to combat evil on its own ground. And yes, you can also change things with a single trigger pull."

Jake stands up and starts pacing around the room. He goes to a bookcase, reaches behind a row of Robert B. Parker *Spenser* novels, and pulls out a pack of Marlboros. He walks to the kitchen, lights a cigarette from the stove, and paces some more.

"Those are bad for you," Saul says. "And the smoke is bad for the books. You know this." Jake ignores him.

"An assassin," he says. "You are saying God sent you here to tell me to be an assassin."

"You're still not seeing the big picture," Saul says, exasperated. "But what if He did? God used the Philistines, Assyrians, and Babylonians to chasten Israel. He used Samson, Joshua, and Elijah to destroy Israel's enemies. Were any of these assassins? Were you an assassin when you removed the enemies of your country? But there is more to battling evil men than just killing them."

"What evil men?" Jake asks, confused even more.

"That is something you have to discover on your own," he says, "as well as how best to deal with them. I have nothing more for you."

Jake stares at him for what feels like a long time, but Saul says nothing else. Finally, Jake turns on the television, pushes 'play,' and sits down next to Saul to watch the end of *Seinfeld.*

26

"The Hagiographer"

If Camden thought Sal's religious bookstore idea farfetched, one can only imagine what she would think about the meeting he has arranged for Jake and Saul. Jake had mentioned, only in passing, that it might be a cool idea to be able to interview Saul about the many questions people had asked about him over the centuries, but what writer would be crazy enough to agree to such an interview. Saul loved the idea and pestered him about it constantly. Jake finally relented and asked Sal to arrange a meeting with the only writer he knew who might do it: Max Luther.

Max was an accomplished, even semi-famous novelist who had shown up in Fort Worth very down on his luck. He had spent several months living with Sal and Camden while trying to turn things around and through a series of fortunate events this turnaround had occurred. He now lived in a very nice loft on the south side of downtown in the old TRE building and was once again making his living writing. Sal arranged a meeting at The Daily Grind, knowing that the coffee shop was Max's favorite place to write.

Max is waiting at a table near the back when Sal walks in accompanied by Jake and Saul. Sal sees him and leads the other two over to his table. Max did not get much detail about this meeting, but quickly agreed because of how great Sal has been to him.

"Max," Sal says. "Great to see you again. You need to come by the store more often. You know Jake already, and this is his…well, maybe I better let him explain who this is."

Max isn't sure what to think of this introduction, but before he can even say hello the older man is dragging Jake to the counter, demanding coffee. Sal takes a seat but says nothing further.

The two men return with their coffee, the older one clearly pleased. Jake sets a third cup down in front of Sal, who accepts it gratefully. Jake looks at the older man as if he thinks he is going to begin talking, but when he doesn't he turns his attention to Max.

"Let me get straight to it," he says. "You're the only writer I know personally, though I'll admit right up front that I haven't read any of your stuff, no offense intended."

"None taken," Max says. He appreciates the guy's honesty. Nothing is worse than someone acting like they'd read your work when they obviously hadn't; it was embarrassing for everyone involved.

"And Ortiz tells me that you're open to taking on interesting topics," Jake continues, "like novels with him as the hero."

"He is a most interesting character," Max replies, "though we haven't been able to get together enough to finish anything."

"He has a lot of irons in the fire," Jake says. "In the meantime, my friend here has a story he wants to share, so we thought it might be good to get the two of you together. This is Saul. You might know him better as the Apostle Paul."

Saul is in mid-sip when Jake says this, but rather than putting down the cup he simply arches his eyebrows in greeting. At least it seems like a greeting to Max, though he has no clue why this would be. When Saul finally puts the cup down, he stares hard at Max, much too hard, Max thinks. It makes him uncomfortable, as if this old man can actually see his secrets.

"I have a message of sorts that I need to share, and some misconceptions to clear up," Saul says, "and these two gentlemen have agreed to find me a hagiographer."

"A what?" Max asks. He knows the word, but for the life of him cannot recall what it means.

"A hagiographer is someone who writes about the lives of the saints," Sal explains. "Just hear him out; it will be worth it, I think. We'll leave you two to talk; see you in an hour or so."

Without another word, Sal and Jake get up and walk out, leaving Max alone with Saul. Saul says nothing, seemingly content to sip his coffee and wait for Max to begin.

"You really think you're the Apostle Paul?" Max finally asks.

"Don't you?" Saul answers.

"Of course not; it's simply not possible. And I'd be shocked if Sal believed a word of it either. My bet is that he's just humoring his friend."

"Then why would he bring me to you, if I'm nothing more than a fraud?"

"I don't know," Max says. "Maybe he thinks I can turn it into a good story. I have written some weird shit over the years." He expects the 'saint' to object to the profanity, but he doesn't.

"True," Saul agrees, "at least with regard to the weird things you've written. Like that sequel to *On the Road* you wrote with yourself as the main character. Why did you never publish that?"

"Copyright issues," Max replies without thinking. "Besides, that one was so weird even Kerouac –" he stops mid-sentence, his hand frozen a few inches from his coffee cup. Saul smiles broadly.

"How…how did you know about that?" Max asks, glancing around to make sure no one else can hear them.

"What do you mean? You did write it, didn't you? I think you were going to call it *Beat in Brooklyn* or something like that. Not a very catchy title, if you ask me."

"I did write it," Max answers. "But no one ever saw it, or ever even knew about it. Not my editor, not my agent, not even my second ex-wife, nobody. I banged it out in a cocaine-induced haze over a two-week stretch and then burned the manuscript. There is no way you could have known."

"There are a few select things I am allowed to know in order to convince the skeptical," he says. "Would you be kind enough to get me another coffee?"

Max gets up and orders two more coffees, then sits back down with his head still spinning. *Who is this guy?*

"What exactly is it that you want me to write about you?" he asks, hoping to move on before Saul drops another bombshell on him. He is still not convinced this is the man who wrote half the New Testament, but he is definitely no ordinary lunatic.

"I want to set the record straight," Saul replies. "For two thousand years people have been twisting my words and misrepresenting what I said and who I was in order to fit their own agendas. Surely you, as a fellow writer, can see how infuriating that would be."

Max nods; he can't argue with that point, though he has never in his life thought of St. Paul as a "fellow writer."

"They pay more attention to a handful of letters I wrote than to the things Jesus actually taught. It makes me sorry I ever took up a pen."

"I can understand that," Max says. "But a hagiography, if I remember right, is supposed to build up the person you're writing about to saint status. It sounds like you want exactly the opposite."

"I want the truth to be told," Saul says firmly.

"What is truth?" Max asks, trying not to laugh.

"Well played. Quoting Pilate so I will know you're not as biblically illiterate as you might seem.

"I have my moments." Max is silent for a while, considering how to approach this project, if at all. "The problem," he says, "is that I'm no theologian, and when you add in the fact that no one is going to believe you are who you say you are, this can't work either as biography or even straight non-fiction."

"Then write it as a story, a novel," Saul says. "That's what you're good at, right?"

"Sometimes," Max says under his breath. "Ok, and I am absolutely not agreeing to anything yet, but let me ask a couple of things that I personally have wondered about that most readers would also want to know. That might be the best place to start."

"Fire away," Saul says, taking another deep drink of his coffee.

"I suppose we should start with the whole first chapter of Romans controversy."

"You mean the part that supposedly proves God hates gays?" Saul asks. "I didn't write it."

"Excuse me?" Max says, taken aback.

"Nope, wasn't me."

"Yes it was."

"Look," Saul says as if trying to reason with an inebriated imbecile, "if you read Romans 16:22 it says 'I, Tertius, who wrote down this letter.' He was my scribe, and he added verses 24 through 27 of chapter one without my knowledge. I didn't find out about it until much later."

"Why would he do that?"

"He was madly in love with a girl in Corinth, and believed they would be married. Then she ran off with a priestess from the Temple of Aphrodite. He apparently took it pretty hard."

"You're joking," Max says.

"I'm joking about not writing it," he says, "but not about what happened to poor Tertius. He was a wreck for months after that."

"Look," Saul continues, "God loves all of his children, including homosexuals. That love does not mean that He condones sin, and sin is anything contrary to how we were created to love, worship, glorify Him. This was never an issue before you people created the cult of the individual during your Me Generation/Sexual Revolution. Looking back, I do wish I hadn't put the homosexual part first in the list of sins, because greed, malice, envy, murder, and the like also continue unabated, yet hardly get mentioned. The controversy raging now is simply another case of people focusing on the sins they don't commit. Some have made homosexuality the unforgiveable sin, while others tear out the whole chapter because they don't like it. Neither way is good."

"Interesting viewpoint," Max says, scribbling furiously in his journal. "So what is your feeling about the issue today?"

"I am not going there," Saul says, shaking his head. "The whole point of this discussion is to get people to quit looking to me for answers and look to what Jesus said."

"Ok," he says, a bit disappointed. What about the claim that you are a misogynist?"

"I don't know what that means," Saul says.

"It means you hate women."

"Ah," Saul replies, then leans back in his chair as if remembering something from long ago. "I will admit that this belief is at least partly my own fault. Though I took great pains to show that all of God's children were equal in his sight, and all important to the work of the kingdom, I may have sometimes come across a bit harshly to women."

"A bit, yeah. And why was that?" Max asks.

"In all honesty, I may have been a little bitter toward women, given that my wife had just left me."

"You had a wife? You never mention having a wife in your letters."

"Don't be stupid," Saul says. "Of course I had a wife. I was a Pharisee, and over 30 years old. Every man over 30 had a wife, especially Pharisees. She divorced me when I became a follower of The Way, unable to believe that Jesus was our long-awaited Messiah. Still no excuse for being harsh to all women."

"I'm sorry," Max says, and means it. After four divorces, he can sympathize. "Did you have any children?"

"I did," Saul says, with a faraway look in his eyes. "A son; he stayed with his mother, and I never saw him again."

"Is that why you had such an attachment to Timothy, if you don't mind me asking?"

"You know more about me than you initially let on," Saul says. "Yes, that was a big reason why, yes. In addition to a fellow worker, it was as if the Lord had given me back a son, if only a son in the Spirit. I have endured much for the Gospel, much more than just shipwreck and prison and floggings. In the end, those were the easy parts."

"Ok, here's one that's I've wondered about, having grown up Episcopalian," Max says.

"I'm listening."

"You condemned rituals," Max says, "so does that condemn all denominations today that have rituals, the Catholics, Orthodox, Anglican, and churches like that?"

"I'm a Jew, son. I love the rituals...even now they mean something to me. My point was about *empty* rituals. I did not mean that all rituals are bad, just the empty ones. Seemed pretty obvious to me when I wrote it."

"When you put it like that it does seem obvious," Max admits.

"One last question for now," Max says, "then I will need to read more, if we continue. You told me earlier that you almost wish you hadn't written any of your letters. But surely there is one New Testament letter you would recommend to people, one that sums up everything they need to know. Besides the gospels, of course."

"There is indeed," Saul says. "It's the one written by James."

"But," Max says, "and I do remember this, you and James disagreed on the issue of faith and works."

"Did not."

"Sure you did," Max insists. "You said faith was what mattered, that works could not save you. James said faith without works was dead."

"We were talking about two sides of the same coin," Saul says calmly. "Works without faith are simply that, good deeds. Faith without works isn't really faith, it's just lip service. Don't forget that I also wrote that you should work out your faith with fear and trembling. I stole that one from the Buddha, by the way. He said it to his disciples on his deathbed."

As he writes this down in his journal, Sal and Jake reappear, as if on cue. They set a time to meet again to continue the interview, and Sal, Jake, and Saul exit the coffee shop, leaving Max to ponder what exactly he has gotten himself into.

27

"Career Counseling"

Sal slips down the short alley off 8th Street just past Houston. He moves quickly down a flight of concrete steps that lead to what at first glance appears to be the basement of the Robber Baron's Restaurant directly above. In reality, it is a completely separate establishment, by night the raucous Bop Jazz Lounge and by day the quietest place to drink in town. Once inside his eyes struggle to adjust to the dim lighting, but after a moment he sees Jake and Ortiz seated at a booth in the far corner.

There had been a time when Sal spent the better part of his day in places like this, but since taking over the bookstore he only drank during the day occasionally. His definition of occasionally differed somewhat from Camden's, but she had been an accountant after all. He is not at all surprised that Ortiz suggested a mid-afternoon beverage, but does find it odd that Jake is here as well, a half-finished beer in front of him. Sal didn't think preachers were allowed to drink during the day.

"Salvatore," Ortiz says when he sees Sal approach, his ever-present grin widening. "I am pleased that you could join us. My brother Jake is struggling with a dilemma and your counsel would be most appreciated."

If he needs my counsel, Sal thinks, *he's in a lot of trouble.* He slides into the booth beside Ortiz; since he has apparently been invited in order to talk with Jake he wants to be able to look him in the eye. He is barely settled before a haggard waitress of indeterminate age sets a mug of beer in front of him and hurries away. He takes a cautious sip, happily finds it to be a good local microbrew, and looks at Jake.

"Problems with the prophet?" he asks, referring to Saul.

"The *saint,*" Ortiz corrects him sharply. Latin guys tolerate no insolence about their mothers or their saints.

"Not with him personally," Jake answers with a shrug. "I'm actually getting used to having him around."

"So where is the old guy now?" Sal asks Jake.

"Back at my place."

"What's he doing? Praying? Writing more letters?"

"When I left he was Googling himself," Jake replies.

"Seriously?" Sal asks.

"Yep. 'Saul of Tarsus' brings up 357,000 results. 'Apostle Paul' brings up 797,000. He'll be at it for a while."

"Ok. So is it woman trouble then? Heather still mad that you're reading Faulkner?"

"She told you that?" Jake replies.

"Nope. Heard it from Ben. Don't let his Greek god exterior fool you; that boy is a shameless gossip."

"To be completely honest," Jake says, "I suppose all of it ties together: Saul, Heather, everything else. My problem is that I'm pondering a career change. A big one."

Sal had not expected that.

"And you're coming to me for advice? Good Lord why?"

Jake and Ortiz both stare at him as if he has a thumb growing out of the middle of his forehead. He suddenly understands.

"Right," he says. "Because I made the big leap from burglar to bookseller you think I have some insight into what it takes."

Jake nods, and Ortiz motions to the waitress for more pretzels. Sal takes another swig of beer; there is just a hint of cinnamon aftertaste.

"My situation is completely different than yours," Sal continues. "I had to get out of the life before something very bad happened, like death or prison. You have a respectable job, some would call it a calling even."

"Most actually do call it a calling," Jake agrees. "But I'm starting to think it's no longer my calling. Or so I have been told by a higher authority."

Sal considers this, then tries to remember all he knows about Jake, which isn't much when you consider they have known each other for over a year. Oddly enough, in spite of their obvious differences, they do have quite a bit in common. Sal decides to start from this common ground.

"This really wouldn't be your first big career change," Sal observes. "It would be your second. Maybe we should start there, because there are some similarities between us."

Jake nods and glances at Ortiz, unsure where Sal is going with this.

"You were part of a large, disciplined organization in the Army, much like I was with, well, you know who I was with. But you were a sniper, which left you on your own -"

"Not on his own," Ortiz interjects. "I was with him the whole way."

"Of course," Sal says. "But in essence you were separate from the larger group, basically your own boss. Same with me. And the jobs were high-risk, just like mine."

"Except that if you got caught you went to a nice comfy jail," Jake replies. "Whereas if Lou and I got caught, we came home in a bag, if at all."

"Right," Sal says. "Your gig was more high-risk. But that's the key I think. You, my friend, are an adrenaline junkie. And preaching doesn't come close to producing the high you're used to."

Jake starts to answer but Sal cuts him off.

"It's probably not even your fault," he continues. "I think it's hereditary. My old man was constantly chasing thrills at the track, the casino, backroom dice games. Hell, he died of a heart attack at a roulette wheel in Atlantic City when his number finally hit."

Jake and Ortiz gaze at him, uncertain if he's serious.

"True story," he assures them. "Mom was angrier that the casino wouldn't pay her what he won than that he had keeled over so publicly, the damn Harpy."

"My dad wasn't a gambler," Jake says.

"Of course he was," Sal says, "he was a legendary gambler. He was The Shamrock, the New York Irishman who set his sights on taking a town from the Texas good old boys and running it like his own little kingdom. Hard to imagine a bigger gamble than that."

Ortiz nods at this. "Mr. Donovan was a great man," he agrees.

"I still don't see -" Jake says.

"Here is where we diverge," Sal says, cutting him off again. "You inherited something in spades that I only have in the presence of a nun: guilt. You can't really help it either; it's cultural. The Irish feel guilty about everything."

"He is right about that, my friend," Ortiz says to Jake, motioning to the waitress for refills.

"Maybe," Jake mutters.

"And that guilt," Sal continues, "guilt over all those guys on the other end of your rifle, even though it was your job, even though part of you enjoyed it, *especially* because part of you enjoyed it, is what sent you on a search for God, meaning, whatever."

"Nothing wrong with searching for God," Jake says. "You should try it sometime."

"Not my style," Sal replies. "But it is yours, and you threw yourself into it 100 percent. Now you're thinking maybe that reaction was the wrong one. It may even be that having this alleged apostle around has finally made that clear to you."

Jake stares into his glass, and Sal wonders if maybe he has gone too far with this. After all, he doesn't know Jake all that well, and here he is acting like some kind of therapist. Jake finally looks up at him.

"Perhaps," he says reluctantly. "The problem is that, unlike you, I don't have a burning passion to replace it with. You had bookselling as your exit from your old life. I don't have anything."

Sal considers this as the waitress sets down more drinks. He has no doubt that Ortiz could pull Jake into any number of questionable pursuits, but the guilt would certainly kick in again. He also assumes that Jake had long ago made the decision to step away from the life his father led, which made anything illegal a non-starter.

"I am sorry, my brother," Ortiz says finally, "but that is simply not true."

Jake and Sal stare at him, both surprised by his tone, which falls somewhere between drill sergeant and school teacher.

"Say again?" Jake says.

"You heard me, bro," Ortiz says. "You know what you, what *we* could be doing that is perfect for both of us."

"For the last time, I'm not becoming a televangelist, Luis," he says firmly.

"I am not talking about that nonsense," Ortiz says sharply. "You know perfectly well what I am talking about. The Saint told you as much."

Jake sighs heavily. "Not this again, Lou," he says.

"Yes, this again. I cannot fathom why you continue to resist it."

Sal is totally confused now. The conversation has obviously moved into very personal territory; for a moment he considers just leaving, but before he can Ortiz explains.

"Salvatore," he says, "Jake has known what to do for years, but he is a stubborn Mick. He loves to travel the world, so he organizes mission trips that only partially fill that need. He wants to feel like he is doing something for the greater good – a trait of his I have labored for years to eradicate, with no success – so he tries to save every so-called sinner he meets. And he likes having food and a roof over his head, so he must earn a living while doing these things. The solution to all of this has been before us for years, yet still he resists."

"It's a crazy idea," Jake says. "And the way you want to do it makes it borderline illegal."

Ortiz laughs loudly at this, which forces Jake's somber expression to vanish.

"Sal," he says after regaining his composure, "my dear friend here has never grasped the nuance between illegal and immoral. Laws, correct or not, are set in stone; ethics are in the eye of the beholder."

"I get that," Sal says. "But what the hell are you two talking about?"

"It all started in Sarajevo," Ortiz says. "We were not deployed in an 'official' capacity yet, at least not with the UN forces, but Jake and I found ourselves there just as the siege of the city began. We had no authorization to engage in any way, we were only supposed to observe, but then the Serbs started shelling the National Library."

Sal remembered the stories, mostly of atrocities committed on both sides. But the destruction of the National Library had particularly stuck in his mind. Hundreds of thousands of priceless books and original manuscripts destroyed in one night of madness, all in an attempt by the Serbs to erase the history of the Bosnian Muslims.

"What did you do?" Sal asks. "I read that people risked their lives to save as many books as they could from the flames, but what could you two have done against the whole Serbian Army?"

Jake really didn't want to answer this, in fact would never have admitted they'd even been in Sarajevo, but Ortiz loved telling the stories. Before he can stop him, Ortiz plunges on.

"We took out a few of them when we could, but that is not the point I am making. Jake and I saw some Serb officers making off with several crates *before* the shelling started. We followed them and separated them from their ill-gotten loot."

"Separated?"

"With extreme prejudice," Ortiz says with a wicked grin that reminds Sal he is a man for whom violence is simply part of who he is.

"What was in the crates?" he asks.

"Illustrated manuscripts," Jake answers. "15th or 16th century. There were a few copies of the Koran, a complete Torah, some Sufi writings. Absolutely beautiful…and priceless."

"Culturally priceless," Ortiz corrects him. "The British Museum paid us a very nice honorarium for rescuing them, much more than the Smithsonian offered."

"And the Russian oligarch paid even more for the one you sold him without my knowledge," Jake says disapprovingly.

"What's the difference?" Sal asks. "Both paid you, and both got something in return. Sounds like straight capitalism to me."

"I knew that you would agree with me, Salvatore," Ortiz says. "You have always struck me as practical man."

"There is a big difference," Jake says. "The British Museum paid a lot, but they returned the manuscripts to the Bosnians after the war, which they told us upfront they would do. The Russian has his in a dacha outside St. Petersburg."

"Antiquities do not all belong in a museum, Jake, as I am sure Sal would agree."

"I actually do agree," Sal says, "at least up to a point. But I still don't see what any of this has to do with Jake finding a new career."

Ortiz begins to speak again, but stops. He looks at Jake, and Sal can see the bond that exists between them, forged through years of shared experiences few could ever understand. He wants Jake to be the one to answer, and finally he does.

"Ortiz believes we can be modern-day treasure hunters, but in a unique way," he says. "Instead of diving for shipwrecks or digging for artifacts, we would build an elite team that would either prevent the theft or destruction of antiquities, or would recover them after such a theft. For a hefty price." *Battling evil men*, he thinks.

Sal doesn't respond immediately. At first glance, it seems like a ridiculous idea, though totally in keeping with

Ortiz' larger-than-life image of himself. But after some thought he must admit it is a service that is sorely needed in many parts of the world, at least if you care about things like books, artifacts, history. It was only a few years ago that the Iraqi National Museum had been looted after Saddam fell from power; few, then or now, seemed to care that thousands of years of Iraqi heritage had been left completely unprotected and was now lost forever.

"It's a long way from preaching," Sal says finally. "But it's an interesting idea, and I think it fits you more than what you're doing now."

Ortiz beams at this, but Jake shakes his head in disbelief.

"This was not what I had in mind when I asked you to meet me." he says.

"What were you expecting?"

Jake wipes some condensation from his glass before answering. It sounds a little silly to him now.

"I was actually considering opening a used bookstore in Arlington," he says. "There's a vacant building across from The Blarney Stone that would be perfect. Then I heard about your book town idea and shifted the plan to downtown Fort Worth. I figured you could give me some advice about it."

Whatever Sal had expected him to say, this certainly wasn't it. He knew Jake was an avid reader; it was one of several things that attracted Heather to him. But a bookseller? He quickly decides to give him a brutally honest answer.

"You're no bookseller, Jake," he says. "You would be bored out of your mind inside of a month, being stuck in a shop all day, every day. Hell, it's hard for me, and I've wanted to do this since I was a little kid."

"Yet you've made the adjustment," Jake counters.

"Barely. And I have something you don't: a partner than knows the business side, and the best staff around. Without Cam's accounting background, Julia's organizational skills, and Heather and Jacob's knowledge, we never would have survived the first year. And again, you're no shopkeeper."

Ortiz nods. His arms are folded across his massive chest and he takes in their exchange like a Buddha watching two disciples debate the meaning of nothingness.

"A wise assessment, Salvatore," he says. "You see, Jake, even those who do not know you well know you well enough."

"What the hell does that even mean, Lou?" Jake laughs.

"It means, my dear friend, that whether you are ready to admit it or not, we are back in business."

"One thing concerns me about your plan, Ortiz," Sal says. "Wouldn't starting this kind of business put you on that ass-monkey Cosgrove's radar even more than usual?"

Special Agent Dalton Cosgrove is with the Department of Homeland Security, and has been after Ortiz for some time now, not because of his less than legal activities, but because of his ongoing efforts toward Puerto Rican independence. These efforts have not always followed a path approved by the United States government.

"Most likely," Ortiz replies. "But I enjoy my repartee with Agent Cosgrove. For example, while talking on one of my cell phones that I know he monitors, I mentioned to a friend that there was an important shipment coming into Uzbekistan next week. I imagine our good friend is on a plane even as we speak."

Sal thinks this wraps the afternoon's discussion up about as well as one could hope, so he stands, thanks them for the drinks, and heads back to the shop. He is thankful that he found his own calling, even if he does occasionally still want to rob the jewelry store down the street.

28

"Sister Stores"

If Sal thought he had heard the last of a bookstore idea involving Jake Donovan, he was quite wrong. Even more surprising is the fact that it is Ortiz who approaches him with, to put it mildly, a radical idea. He springs this on Sal one afternoon over Irish nachos and beer at the Blarney Stone.

"Sal, my friend," he says, "Jake and I have decided to join your campaign of literary conquest."

"I'm not sure the book town idea is really going anywhere," Sal replies. "It's cool having more bookstores, but it doesn't really give me anything to do besides some promotion and such, and Julia is better at that. Besides, I thought you two were going to travel the world saving antiquities from destruction."

"We are indeed, but we need a base of operations. A place that doesn't draw unwanted attention, so that we can conduct our main business in anonymity."

"In other words," Sal say, "you need a front."

Ortiz smiles broadly and nods.

"It is refreshing being able to speak with someone who understands the realities of the world," he says. "But it is much more than a front. It will be a real business in its own right, and so unique I fear it will become much more famous than your Last Word. Furthermore, it will be a family affair."

"I hope that's family with a small *f*, Lou," Sal replies, eliciting raucous laughter from Ortiz.

"A bit of both, I suppose. All of the Donovans will be a part of this endeavor."

"All? As in Jake and his brother Eddie?" Eddie owns the Blarney Stone and does his best to hold on to the few remaining pieces of his late father's criminal empire.

"And Kathleen," Ortiz says. "Their sister, whom you have yet to meet, whom I have known as a sister myself for decades, who is more beautiful than Aphrodite and more ruthless than Mars."

"Lovely,' Sal says, motioning for another beer. "You and three Donovans. What can possibly go wrong?"

"Indeed!" Ortiz exclaims. "We have decided on sister stores that will be side-by-side and will each offer something so unique as to be immune to failure."

"That is a bold statement. Please elaborate."

"I can give only the most basic information at the moment, but one will be a bookstore and wine bar."

"A good idea," Sal says, "though in Fort Worth don't you think beer would be better? A bookstore and microbrewery perhaps?"

"No," he replies. "A wine bar, with books that appeal to women who drink wine in bars."

"Way to target your market, Lou."

Ortiz ignores this.

"The second store will be adjacent to the first, and will appeal to the husbands of the aforementioned ladies, as well as to men such as Jake and myself."

"Let me guess: a strip club with a magazine stand."

Ortiz pauses, stares hard at Sal, then removes a small notebook from his pocket. Sal watches, his view upside down, as Ortiz scribbles "strip club with magazines." He replaces the notebook and continues.

"No," he says. "A bookstore and gun shop."

Sal isn't sure he heard correctly; he hopes he didn't.

"Say again, Lou?"

"A bookstore and gun shop," he repeats. "The adventure tales of our youth, Jules Verne, Edgar Rice Burroughs, and the like, hard-boiled crime novels, and so forth, along with a finely curated selection of quality firearms."

"No offense, but that's nuts."

"In fact, my friend, it makes perfect sense. We will have a legitimate reason for owning large quantities of arms and ammunition for our real venture, as well as secure place to store them."

"Getting permits from the city alone will take forever."

"Not for me. I have certain relationships with certain municipal employees that enable me to expedite almost anything."

A long silence follows, finally broken by Ortiz.

"Kathleen and Eddie will run the stores when Jake and I are otherwise engaged," he says, "and all will run smoothly. And Salvatore, the names of the stores are the best part. In fact, they have 'franchise' written all over them."

"I'm almost afraid to ask, but what are the names?"

"You know that I am a music fan, yes?"

"Yes."

"And that the public loves a play on words, yes?"

"Yes."

"The two stores will be called, respectively, 'Wine and Proses," and 'Guns 'N Proses.'"

Sal is stunned; the names are brilliant, and he says so. Ortiz simply nods.

"You'll get sued if you use their logo," he says, a smile spreading across his face as he pictures it. "Axl Rose is very litigious."

"Axl is no problem," Ortiz says. "It's Slash that worries me. And one more thing; we will have an indoor range where people can hone their shooting skills day or night."

"That's one benefit," Sal says, "I need to get in as much practice as I can just in case any more of your crew stop by the store."

29

"No Good at Goodbye"

Jake is surprised to wake the next morning and not smell coffee brewing; since he had begun staying there Saul was always the first one up, three cups ahead of Jake by the time he dragged himself out of bed. Maybe the old guy wasn't feeling well.

Jake makes coffee before knocking on the door to Saul's room, assuming that even if he is on death's door he would want some. *Can he actually die?* Jake wonders as he knocks softly. No answer. He knocks more loudly. Nothing. He turns the knob and silently opens the door far enough to stick his head inside.

The blinds are open and sunlight is streaming into the empty room. The bed is made, the desk is clear, and Saul is gone. Jake wonders if he just went out for a morning walk or something, but it doesn't feel like that. The vacancy of the room feels final. Ignoring the freshly brewed coffee he throws on his clothes from the previous night and rushes from the apartment. He has no idea where to look – the diner where they first met? the park? the bookstore? – but knows that he absolutely must find Saul.

Down in the street he scans all directions, but other than a few passing cars there is no one in sight. On impulse, he decides to check The Last Word first, even though they don't open for another hour. Something, whether instinct or intuition he is not sure, tells him that is where he needs to go.

At roughly the same time Jake is walking from his loft, Sal and Camden are getting the store ready for another day of bookselling.

"What do you think about all this, Cam?" Sal asks.

"About what?"

"This whole deal with Saul," Sal says.

Camden doesn't respond immediately; in fact, she is silent for so long that Sal starts to wonder if she has heard him. When she finally does speak, her tone is more serious than he expected.

"I wouldn't have any trouble believing it was the *ghost* of St. Paul," she says. "I know that sounds crazy…whoever heard of seeing the ghost of a saint? But in England, with hundreds upon hundreds of years of history surrounding you at every turn, ghosts aren't a ridiculous notion."

"Jacob Marley and Scrooge's three visitors," Sal says, almost to himself.

"Right," Camden says. "But the bodily return of a saint? That seems quite unlikely."

"Unlikely?" Sal repeats. "That's an odd choice of words."

"I don't think so. When have you ever heard of it happening before, not counting the visions people occasionally have of the Virgin Mary? And seriously Sal, if God *was* going to send St. Paul back to earth in the 21st century, do you really think he would send him to Fort Worth, and to Jake of all people?"

She had a point there. Fort Worth clearly wasn't Jerusalem or Rome or Canterbury, and Jake wasn't the Pope or Billy Graham. Still…

"I have spent some time with the guy," he says, "and he's pretty convincing."

"A lot of schizophrenics are," she replies. "I had a great-uncle who was convinced he was Sherlock Holmes. Dressed like him and everything. And Holmes is fictional. So there you have it."

So there you have it. This is the phrase Camden uses when she believes her argument is unassailable. Sal has heard it many times.

"It would be pretty cool if it really was him," Sal says. "Even you have to admit that."

"Of course it would be cool," she says. "It would be beyond cool. It would be a miracle, though I have trouble believing in those as well."

"Yet every year you have faith that Arsenal will win the Premier League."

"I've seen them do that before," she says proudly. "And will see them do it again. I may even live to see England win the World Cup again. But a saint who has browsed my shelves? That's a bridge too far for me."

"I suppose," Sal says. "It would be really cool though."

There is a rapping on the front door, and Sal looks up to see a barista from The Daily Grind; he is waving an envelope at him. Jake walks to the door and opens it.

"What's up?" he asks.

"Max asked me to deliver this to you," the kid says. "He also said you'd give me 20 bucks."

"Nice try," Sal says, snatching the envelope from the kid's hand and then locking the door again. He opens it and removes the single sheet of paper inside. He can feel small indentations on the back of the sheet; this was typed on a real typewriter, and he only knows one person who still uses a manual typewriter.

Sal quickly scans the page, a smile creeping across his face in spite of himself. Camden walks over to him, and he hands the note to her without a word. After reading it, she smiles as well. But before either of them can comment, there is a loud pounding on the front door of the shop. Sal looks up, expecting an insistent early-bird customer.

But it is not a customer. It's Jake, and his expression is so frantic that Camden immediately assumes someone has died. Sal unbolts the door and Jake rushes in, nearly knocking him over in the process.

"Saul's gone!" he shouts. He looks from Sal to Camden, expecting their shock to match his, but curiously it does not. Sal simply nods, while Camden pats him on the shoulder. She then hands him the sheet of paper. He looks down at it, bewildered, and begins to read.

Sal, Camden, and Jake,

I am writing this for both of us, because Saul says he is frankly sick and tired of writing letters, which I guess is understandable. Neither of us is any good at goodbyes, but we couldn't just disappear without a word, so here are a few. During one of our marathon interviews for the hagiography we discussed the possibility that it was time to move on, and that it might be fun to have a partner on the road. The deal was sealed when we learned that Velvet Revolver is playing in Seattle next week…for some reason Saul is fascinated by Slash. Anyway, we both want to thank you for everything, Saul for believing him, and me for giving me back my voice. I am sure we'll meet up down the line sometime.

And Sal, nice job getting the book town started, but Mr. Moriarty is out of the hospital, feeling much better, and has a quest for you. Go see him.

Keep people reading.

Max and Saul

Max has signed his name normally, but Saul had signed his "Paul," and in parentheses had added "see what large letters I use to write this in my own hand." Jake laughs when he reads this.

"An inside joke?" Sal asks.

"Something he wrote in one of his New Testament letters," Jake replies. Sal snickers at this. "You still don't believe was really the Apostle, do you?" Jake asks.

"I think it's extremely unlikely," Sal answers. "After all, there's very little of what he said that can't be explained in one way or another. I'm amazed you weren't more skeptical."

Jake looks to Camden for support, but she merely shrugs.

"I never really bought into his story either," she says, almost apologetically. "It just didn't seem…logical."

"He told me you would be hard to convince," Jake says, turning to face Sal again. "So he left a message that I was supposed to give you when I thought the time was appropriate."

"And that time is now?" Sal asks, suppressing another laugh.

"Seems so. He told me to ask you if it was harder than usual doing the Ithaca job since you were wearing a tuxedo?"

"Say again?" Sal asks, staring at Jake, dumbfounded. He is not laughing anymore.

"The infamous Ithaca heist," Jake repeats. "Saul said you were wearing a tux."

"There is no way he could have known that," Sal says, barely above a whisper. "No one knew that."

"He knew, or else it was one hell of a good guess. So what do you think of him now?"

Sal doesn't answer; there is no answer that makes any sense to him now. Camden tactfully changes the subject.

"What about you, Jake?" she asks. "Are you going to be okay now that your friend is gone?"

Jake nods. "I'll be fine," he says. "I'll miss our conversations, but I suppose he accomplished what he came for."

"Which was?" she asks, not yet knowing about his imminent career change.

"Putting me back on the right track," he says.

Thirty miles east of Amarillo, the Greyhound bus roars across the empty west Texas plain. A man with a portable typewriter case on the floor between his feet snores softly, his head against the window. In the aisle seat next to him, an older man with bushy white eyebrows is deep in conversation with a college-age boy across the narrow aisle.

"But how can you be so certain that Paul's thorn in the flesh wasn't something of a sexual nature?" he insists. "He did talk a lot about sex."

"Apparently much more than he should have," Saul replies. "But that was not his thorn."

"Then what was it?"

Saul leans across the aisle, beckoning the young man closer. He whispers something in his ear, and his eyes widen in disbelief. Saul nods once, then leans back in his seat and closes his eyes, allowing the hum of the tires to lull him into peaceful slumber.

Acknowledgements

Thanks to everyone who played a part in bringing this book to life, and a special thanks to all the friends, family, and readers who made the real-life The Last Word possible, if only for a season.

Thanks to Courtney, Claudia, and Sophia, who proofed the final draft.

Once again, all my love to my daughters, who get mentioned in both the front and the back of this book. I've said it before and I'll say it again: it's more than you expected and less than you deserve.

Finally, thanks to my sister, Indi Butler, who read the first draft and left the most hilarious notes. You were there from the beginning, and you live on in these pages as much as Sal or Camden or Ortiz. I'll see you on the far shore.

Paul Combs is a writer living in the not always literary state of Texas. His ultimate goal (besides being a roadie for the E Street Band) is to make reading, writing, and books in general as popular in Texas as high school football. It may take a while.

He has written two previous novels, *The Last Word* and *Writer in Residence*.